GET OGRE YOURSELF

A PARANORMAL MYSTERY ADVENTURE

MONSTERS OF JELLYFISH BEACH 3

WARD PARKER

MAD MANGROVE MEDIA, LLC

CONTENTS

CHAPTER 1
ANGLING TO BE MURDERED

I awoke to deep, feral growls in my bedroom.

A werewolf was at the foot of my bed.

No, it couldn't be. I did have an appointment today with a werewolf patient for a deworming treatment, but it was a home-health visit at the werewolf's home, not here at mine.

And the growls weren't quite right. They were low and husky, not the sharp, guttural rumble of a werewolf. The growl had to be coming from one of my cats, since there were no other creatures capable of such a sound.

Unless I was still asleep and was hearing my own snores.

This time, hissing punctuated the growls. Yes, they were coming from a cat. And now, they were in stereo, meaning both Brenda and Bubba were upset about something.

When you're involved with as many supernatural creatures as I am, any intruder in your home was potentially fatal.

As I began casting a protection spell, more growling and

hissing broke out on the floor near the foot of my bed. The sounds were desperate, angry, and fearful.

"Will you guys knock it off?" said a voice in a New York accent. "I'm trying to get some sleep here."

"Tony? Is that you?" I asked.

"Yes, it's me. Tell your cats to lose the territorial attitude. They know who I am."

"You're supposed to sleep in the garage."

"I'm an iguana. I'm cold-blooded. It's freaking freezing out there. I hate these Florida cold fronts. It's still autumn. It shouldn't be this chilly. I've had good friends go into cold shock on mornings like this and fall out of trees. Humans think it's raining frozen iguanas. My best friend, Pete, fell from a tree, was taken home by a human, and turned into stew."

Tony was, as far as I knew, the only talking iguana in Jellyfish Beach. He'd been given to me to serve as my witch's familiar. He was an ancient spirit, most recently inhabiting the body of a Cavalier King Charles Spaniel before being reincarnated as a common green iguana.

"Do you mind if I sleep on the end of your bed?" he asked.

"That's really the cats' territory."

"Looks like they believe this rug next to your bed is their territory, too. Come on, you furry freaks, give a guy a break."

Brenda hissed, Bubba yowled, and Tony yelped in pain.

"Stop it, you psychos!"

Suddenly, tumbling bodies thudded on my hardwood floor, mixed with growls, hisses, and shrieks. A flailing lizard tail hit my nightstand.

I steadied the lamp that sat on it and turned it on. Two gray tabbies disappeared under the bed, and a four-foot-long iguana trotted from the bedroom, emitting more curse words than ever heard at a New York Mafia meeting.

Man, there was no way I'd be able to get back to sleep. Rest constantly eluded me in the weird lifestyle I'd chosen for myself. I no longer worked the graveyard shift as a home-health nurse for vampires and other supernatural creatures, instead working normal hours with Luisa at the Jellyfish Beach Mystical Mart and Botanica. Yet, I had supernatural patients, whom I still saw on a part-time basis, constantly throwing off my body clock.

Plus, I stupidly agreed to get involved in investigations for the botanica's customers and for the Friends of Cryptids Society of the Americas. These investigations always involved monsters of one sort or another.

And monsters always meant staying up late and losing sleep.

I sighed and got out of bed. Shuffling into the kitchen, I turned on the lights and put on a kettle of water for tea, then turned on the TV to watch the local news.

Jellyfish Beach has its own newspaper, but it's too small to have its own TV stations. We rely on the stations in nearby, slightly larger Mullet City to cover the news throughout Crab County.

You know how local news is: stories about commuting woes, new strip malls, school-board controversies, and some guy turning 100 at the assisted-living community. I wasn't really paying attention to the stories as I brewed my tea.

Until I heard the words "murder" and "Jellyfish Beach."

There were hardly any murders in Jellyfish Beach, at least not actual murders committed by humans. The occasional incident of some poor soul being mauled by an out-of-control werewolf was written off as a dog attack. Only the few of us who knew about monsters suspected that when someone disappeared, they might have been digested.

The humans simply didn't kill each other very often. It wasn't that kind of town. And the supernaturals here were usually careful about not killing humans and drawing attention to themselves.

Apparently, today's victim could be the exception. The newscaster said the deceased was a fisherman named Gerald Holstein, then showed a recent photo of the victim. He looked like your typical crusty old retiree, of which Jellyfish Beach had an abundance.

His body was discovered stuffed in a garbage can at the boat ramp. His boat was found a mile away, having drifted down the Intracoastal Waterway into mangrove trees on the shore. The cause of death was not revealed, though the authorities were certain it was a homicide.

The reporter mentioned this was the brief window in the fall when red snapper could legally be harvested offshore. He said Holstein had more than the legal limit of the fish in his cooler, which was found sitting beside the garbage can.

The weather woman came on to talk about the cold front, and I stopped paying attention. I thought about the rules and regulations of fishing meant to preserve healthy populations of the various species. Matt had told me he'd recently been assaulted at the beach when he'd caught a snook, unaware the season had closed the day before. He was hit in the head from behind and never saw his attacker. Planning to keep the fish was an honest mistake, he claimed. He felt lucky he hadn't been killed.

I also remembered that Mrs. Lupis and Mr. Lopez of the Friends of Cryptids Society had warned me about sightings in the area of an unidentified monster not native to Florida.

Could the monster be responsible for killing Holstein?

If so, what exactly was I supposed to do?

My doorbell rang. I rushed to open it and found Mrs. Lupis and Mr. Lopez standing there, silhouetted by the dawn's light.

How did they always mysteriously show up at opportune times like this?

"Good morning," Mr. Lopez said. "We bring information."

"Did you bring donuts, too?"

They ignored me. The two strange agents in gray suits weren't much for humor.

I let them in, and they marched to the kitchen without being led.

"Would you like some tea?" I asked.

"I'm sufficiently caffeinated," Mr. Lopez said.

"With milk and sugar, please," said his partner.

The two sat at my kitchen table, hands folded atop it, and stared at me solemnly while I prepared the tea.

"What information do you have for me?" I asked as I placed the cup, the milk, and the sugar in front of Mrs. Lupis.

"We have credible reports a munuane is in town," she replied.

"A what?"

"An ogre known as the grandfather, or guardian, of the fishes," said Mr. Lopez.

"Its legend comes from the Guahibo people who live in

southern Venezuela and eastern Colombia. Like so many people from those countries, it has moved to South Florida. We don't know why, since it's obviously not coming here for work. We suspect climate change is to blame."

"We have had reports of additional munuanes appearing in the Everglades," Mr. Lopez said, "which makes sense based on its native habitat of forests, jungles, and savannas, as well as freshwater rivers that flow into the tidal estuaries. But it is unusual that this one has appeared on the more heavily populated coast."

"Who gives you the reports?" I asked.

The two exchanged a glance.

"Others like you," Mrs. Lupis said.

"There are others like me?"

"None quite like you," Mr. Lopez said with what I believed was a smile.

"What am I supposed to do?"

"There was a murder," he said. "Perhaps the munuane was responsible."

"It was on the news less than thirty minutes ago. And you guys are here already?"

"We're well connected," Mrs. Lupis said.

"I see."

"Munuanes protect marine life from over-fishing and from cruel handling," Mr. Lopez continued.

"A friend of mine was attacked for harvesting a fish during the closed season for that species. But he wasn't hurt badly. Could the munuane have done that?"

Mr. Lopez nodded. "Somehow, for creatures not known to be especially intelligent, they keep up with all the latest fishing regulations."

"Maybe they have an app."

Again, the two partners were not amused by my joke.

"One reason the munuane is here on the more populated coast is that there is more fishing pressure on the marine populations," Mr. Lopez said.

"You never answered me about what you want me to do."

"Munuanes sometimes attack merely to give a warning, like with your friend," Mr. Lopez said. "Often, however, they kill. According to legend, they use an arrow, but we didn't see that method used on the fisherman yesterday. In any event, this is the classic problem we encounter at the Society—when monsters kill humans. We can't allow the creatures to be discovered by the authorities. It would be, of course, fatal to the creatures and compromise our work at the Society. Also, we don't want to see humans killed. Of course."

"Of course." I had a feeling protecting humans was secondary in importance.

"We need you to discover if there is, in fact, a munuane in the area and if it killed the fisherman," Mrs. Lupis said. "If so, our local enforcer will convince it to change its ways or move to another territory."

"Or it will be put down," Mr. Lopez added. His expression was dark.

The "enforcer" was Angela, whom I'd met recently. She looked every bit the role of librarian at the public library, which was her day job. You would never guess she was an enforcer, but she could be lethal.

"What do munuanes look like?"

"They're ogres," Mr. Lopez said. "Which means they're big

7

and strong, and humans are part of their diet. I assume the reason the fisherman wasn't eaten was to send a warning message."

"They're hairy and don't have eyes in their heads," added Mrs. Lupis. "Their eyes are on their knees and are their most vulnerable points. They're also said to lack teeth, so they bring their victims home and cook them before eating. We don't know how accurate the legends are."

I remembered something from the news. "It was reported that the fisherman had more than the legal limit of red snapper in his cooler. Was that why he was killed?"

"Most likely."

"If, in fact, a munuane was responsible," Mr. Lopez said.

"Okay. If there's one or more munuanes around here, how do I find them?"

"You can violate fishing regulations," Mr. Lopez said with a semblance of a smile. "Then, they will find you."

"They live in the deepest parts of forests along the water," Mrs. Lupis explained. "There aren't many forests left in South Florida, aside from the state and national preserves. That's where you should search."

As if I had time to truck around in the wilderness looking for a legendary monster.

"You know, I have a job at the botanica, plus my home-health nursing. I'm very busy."

"You also have magic," Mrs. Lupis said with a piercing look. "We suggest you use it."

After the partners in gray departed, I called Matt. He mumbled groggily.

"It's time to get up," I said. "Can you meet me for a quick breakfast before you go into the newsroom?"

"I'm going in late today because I have to cover a city council meeting tonight."

"Well, you're already up now. I'll meet you at the usual place in forty-five minutes."

He was late, of course, his hair still wet from his shower and his face unshaven. His smile was strained as he sat across from me on the patio of the café that faced the beach.

After we ordered, I launched right into business.

"I need more details about when you were attacked on the beach. Give me a blow-by-blow account, if you'll pardon the pun."

"It was before dawn during the summer, when snook sometimes show up in the surf, as opposed to just the inlet and Intracoastal Waterway. It didn't even occur to me it was the first day of the closed season." He sounded ashamed.

"I don't care that you did something wrong," I said. "I want to hear about how you were attacked. And why you didn't see your attacker, even though you were in the open with no place for it to hide?"

"You really think a supernatural creature did it?"

I nodded. "An ogre from South America called the munuane. Please go on."

"I have two theories. Someone—or something—came from the road and was good at moving quietly while I was focused on the adrenaline rush of landing the fish. Or someone came from the sea. I thought I saw someone on a paddle board to the south. That was just before hooking the fish, and I didn't look in that direction again. He could have beached his board and snuck around behind me."

I had done more research on munuanes, and I read that the creatures used rafts to travel through the waters of their realm. Using a paddle board would be a fitting contemporary touch.

"You didn't see or hear him come up behind you," I said. "Did you smell anything?"

"Funny you ask. I do remember a funky, unwashed dog smell right before I got clobbered. But I didn't think about it at the time with all the natural ocean scents around me."

"Then what happened? Please be specific."

"I got hammered on the head. I think it was with something wooden because of the sound it made."

"Like a paddle?"

"Maybe. I wasn't knocked unconscious, just stunned. I fell to my knees. This was right after I put the fish in my bag. I heard a splash and saw the fish swimming through the shallows back into the ocean. Obviously, the dude who hit me chucked the fish back. I don't know how he got it out of the bag so quickly. I looked behind me, and there was no one there. That's the end of the story."

"Did you report it to the police?"

"No. Not after I realized I was a day too late to be able to keep the fish. Plus, I had no details about the guy who hit me. I was pretty sure I didn't have a concussion, so I blew it off."

"The munuanes are said to eat their victims, so count yourself lucky."

"Yeah, the bonk on the head was also better than a huge fine from Fish and Wildlife."

"So says the guy on a reporter's salary."

"I take it you're interrogating me because the Friends of Cryptids are interested in this monster? They think it's behind the murder at the boat ramp yesterday?"

"They want me to find out if a munuane did it. But I don't have access to any of the forensic evidence the police collected."

"From what I hear, they gathered very little. And the murder wasn't caught on any of the surveillance cameras at the park."

"Part of my assignment is to find the munuane—and there could be more than one in the area—and document it with photos or video. I don't know how I will find it."

"With magic?"

"That's what my reps from the Society said, but people don't understand. I can't find someone or something just like that." I snapped my fingers. "The locator spell I know requires a physical object containing the psychic energy of the person or creature I'm looking for. I have another spell that sends out sensors randomly based on a mental image I have of the search subject. But I've never seen a munuane—only an illustration someone dreamed up. It would be no better than sending drones over a forest, looking for Bigfoot. Unless I can find a better spell, I'm afraid I'll have to physically search for the creature."

"I'll go with you."

"Thanks, but it will be like the old needle-in-a-haystack cliché."

"It will be more effective if we use bait to lure it," Matt said with a conspiratorial grin.

"You mean fish unethically? That's what Mrs. Lupis and Mr. Lopez suggested."

"Yeah. Or we pretend to."

"You might get eaten this time."

"Unless I can run away faster than you."

CHAPTER 2

HUNTERS WERE HUNTED

George was a long-time patient of mine. He was also an Old World ogre. There were many supernatural creatures who lived in and around Jellyfish Beach, but they didn't congregate in communities the way the retired vampires at Squid Tower and the aging werewolves of Seaweed Manor did. There simply weren't enough members of the other species to form communities of their own.

I had two troll patients who lived, appropriately enough, in condos at the foot of a bridge. They could pass themselves off in public as human—large, lumbering humans—but couldn't go to human doctors without revealing that they were trolls. That's why they needed my services.

It was the same for George, who lived in a golf course community just west of town. He had a convincing story that he once was a defensive tackle with the NFL, which explained his enormous bulk and lack of a discernible neck. His slightly green complexion and pointy ears were harder to explain away.

I met him on his lanai, which faced a lush fairway. We sipped iced tea while he gnawed at a bone that looked like a human femur. I didn't want to know.

"You think, just because I'm an ogre, I would know about this menudo?" he asked in his gruff voice.

"Munuane."

"I met a human once. His name was Dave. Do you know him?"

"I get the point. Sorry. I just don't know many ogres, and I thought you might have some insights about how to find him. I only have his best interests in mind."

"You'll have better luck looking into the indigenous people who named him. Where did you say he was from?"

"Colombia and Venezuela."

"One thing you need to keep in mind is to not rely on the folklore about beings like us to inform your decisions. Even back in the days of yore, hardly any of the folks who sat around the fire and told stories about ogres had ever actually seen one. They're just repeating tales they heard from someone else and putting their own spin on them. A lot of what you'll read about this munololo—"

"Munuane."

"—is just made up. He or she probably has habits more like modern humans," George said as he absentmindedly scrolled through his phone with a thumb half the size of the screen. There were scratches all over it from his long black nails.

"The recurring theme of these legends is that the munuane is the grandfather of the fishes and protector of the waterways. That's why the people I work for think he murdered the fisherman at the boat ramp. And I think he attacked a friend of mine who caught and intended to keep a snook off season."

George shrugged his massive shoulders beneath a tight, green golf polo that went well with his complexion.

"One thing I can say about ogres is that we're very single-minded and determined. If this—whatever's he's called—is out to protect the fish population, nothing's gonna stop him from doing that. And that's difficult with all the humans moving to Florida." He gestured at the homes across the fairway.

"You moved to Florida, too, and bought a house," I reminded him.

"Yeah. Back when it was less crowded. Anyway, don't be surprised if more fishermen end up dead."

George was right. Right after I left the ogre's gated community, my phone rang.

"How close are you to the Wikowackee Preserve?" Matt asked.

"Actually, I'm in the area."

"Go there now. I just heard over my police scanner that the bodies of two fishermen were found. Suspected homicides. I'm on the way."

"Okay. See you there."

The Wikowackee National Wildlife Preserve was an enormous tract of pristine wilderness. You could call it the northern tip of the Everglades, the river of grass that once flowed unimpeded from Central Florida lakes to Florida Bay at the southern tip of the peninsula. The preserve was grasslands and forests carved up by winding rivers and creeks crowded with fish and alligators.

Nothing seemed out of the ordinary as I drove down the entrance road. I passed a group of birdwatchers emerging from a forest trail, laden with binoculars and cameras with telephoto lenses. The turnoff to the visitors' center was to my right, but I saw flashing lights far ahead of me where the road ended at the boat ramps.

I slowed as the asphalt turned into a dirt road. I parked in a sandy parking lot beside a wide creek of dark water with banks of tall grasses. Two dirt ramps to the water were flanked by wooden fishing piers.

Unlike the boat ramp on the Intracoastal where the first body was found, these ramps were remote and closed at night. Here, there was freshwater instead of saltwater, but the purpose was the same: catching fish.

The victims' jon boat had run aground and was surrounded by first responders and crime-scene techs.

I parked and approached the scene until a Crab County Sheriff's deputy waved me away.

"What happened?" I asked.

"Just an accident. There's nothing to see."

"Was it fatal?"

The deputy, a slight Hispanic male, paused, then admitted, "Yeah. Good thing they died in their boat. Usually, when we find deceased fishermen out here, they've been chewed up by gators too badly to tell what happened to them."

"So, what happened to these guys?"

"That has to be determined by the medical examiner."

"Were they beaten to death?" I asked.

"I'm not authorized to say, ma'am. Could you move along, please?"

Matt's beat-up pickup truck clattered into the parking lot in a cloud of dust. He parked near my car and jumped out, striding toward the deputy and me.

"Hey, Alberto!" he said, waving to the deputy. "What do we have here?"

The deputy seemed to recognize Matt, but was unsure until Matt flashed his press ID.

"I'm not authorized to—"

Matt barged past him and gestured for me to follow.

"This is my researcher," Matt explained as we left the deputy in our wake.

The deputy watched us impotently as we approached the crime scene. I had the feeling Matt did this kind of thing all the time.

"Did you hear on the scanner how they died?" I asked Matt.

"They were shot. You told me munuanes shoot their victims with arrows."

"That's just folklore," I said, echoing George. "I'm sure they have adopted modern killing technology."

We wove our way through first responders, who were milling about with no lives to save, and approached the beached boat with two crime-scene techs aboard taking photos. An older, beer-bellied deputy wearing a badge and plain clothes walked up to Matt with authority.

"Who gave you permission to crash my party, Rosen?"

"It's nice to see you, too, Sergeant. What do you make of the scene?"

"We have two victims, both male. Their boat ran aground at high speed about forty minutes ago. Fishermen who were preparing to launch at the ramp ran over and saw the occupants lying prone on the deck."

"They were shot?" Matt asked.

"Looks like gunshots to the head at close range."

"Were they fishing illegally?" I asked.

The detective looked at me like he only just now noticed I was there.

"No. They were hunting gators. We're checking to see if they had permits. Oh, the M.E. is here." The sergeant abruptly turned away and intercepted a middle-aged woman striding from the parking lot to the boat.

"Do you really think this munuane is killing people for violating fishing and hunting regulations?" Matt asked me. "I mean, it seems kind of bureaucratic for a monster to get caught up in enforcing the minutia of the law. I'm a first-time offender, so I just get bonked in the head. Same if your fish is one inch too short. But if it's a more serious offense, you get killed?"

"Yeah, you're probably right. I'm taking the oral legends too literally. Maybe he kills anyone he comes across who is greedy and harvests too many of the same creatures the munuane is hunting. Who knows?"

Matt was watching the medical examiner and sergeant approach the boat.

"Let's get closer and try to overhear."

We walked as casually as we could around the fringes of the personnel on site until we got close enough to the grounded boat that I could see the two bodies on the deck.

The first responders were already returning to their trucks, the crime-scene techs were packing their gear, and two men from the medical-examiner's office were wheeling gurneys toward the boat.

Whenever the breeze shifted in our direction, I heard snippets of conversation. They meant nothing to me until the medical examiner spoke with conviction.

"It wasn't a firearm. They were shot with the bang stick they used for killing gators."

Matt and I looked at each other.

"The munuane has a sense of irony," I said. "Did they ever release the cause of death for the snapper fisherman?"

Matt searched his newspaper archives on his phone.

"Okay, I think I found something . . . ew, gross."

"What?"

"Gerald Holstein was drowned in the half-melted ice of his cooler with all the dead snapper he had caught. Someone must have forced his head in there and held it down. Not a pleasant way to go—drowning in ice water and fish slime."

"Asphyxiated like the fish he caught. More irony."

"Are ogres capable of irony?"

"Why not? If you move from remote jungles to crowded South Florida, you've got to develop a sense of irony just to survive."

"If you were a monster and moved to an unfamiliar area, wouldn't you want to avoid drawing attention to yourself?"

He had a point. I don't know why one or more munuanes moved to Florida—whether it was because of climate change or other reasons—but killing people to send a message would not be a priority.

"If humans did this," I said, "the Friends of Cryptids Society doesn't have to worry about the munuane getting arrested."

"Yeah. You don't need to investigate this, then. Just let the cops find the murderer."

"No, I still have to find the munuane and get photos or videos of it."

"Can't you tell those cryptid creeps to buzz off?"

"Luisa and I are both financially dependent upon them. The botanica doesn't make enough money on its own, and even with my home-health visits on the side, I wouldn't survive without the cryptid creeps. I plan to go with your idea and try to lure the munuane. But I don't want to do it out here with all the alligators and mosquitos."

"Then we'll do it at the north causeway at night. Snook are still out of season, and there's good catch-and-release fishing for them there. Maybe I'll catch one or two. Maybe I'll decide to keep one. We might prove or put to rest the theory that the munuanes punish rule breakers."

THE NORTH CAUSEWAY existed at a point where the Intracoastal Waterway was too wide for a bridge to span it. Decades ago, manmade peninsulas with roads were built jutting out from the opposite shores, leaving a gap at the deepest and most navigable channel. A tall bridge was built to span the gap. The land segments of the causeway were turned into parks, providing lots of waterfront access to the public.

A small fishing pier was also built at the end of the west causeway, extending beneath the tall bridge, taking advantage of its shade. At night, the lights of the bridge spotlighted the water below, attracting fish within easy casting distance from the pier. That was where we went.

I had presumed it would be deserted this late at night and was surprised to find so many people spending their Saturday night at the pier, hidden from view from the bridge. Families with folding chairs, young couples on dates, and the hardcore fishermen that Matt called pier rats lined the railings of the pier, against which they leaned their rods, hoping to catch snapper, sheepshead, and redfish. I hoped everyone would leave soon. I didn't want the munuane to be scared off or, worse, attack an ordinary person.

"This is a good cheap date," I said to Matt.

"It's only cheap if you don't spend too much on live bait."

"You must really impress the girls."

He glared at me. "I don't date. I thought you knew that."

Yes, I did. Matt was waiting for me to come around. I didn't know if I was capable of romantic love anymore. If I ever was, I hoped Matt would be the recipient.

He became all business once he had our lines in the water. I'm not into fishing like Matt is, and he explained he usually only used lures when he fished, but tonight, we would use live bait, under the theory that the more creatures we disrupted, the more likely we would attract the munuane. So, I had a live shrimp on my line, and he had a mullet on his.

"Do you know any spells that could attract fish?" Matt asked.

"Isn't that unsportsmanlike?"

"Heck, yes. We're supposed to be greedy, unethical fishermen who deserve to be punished."

A nearby pier rat, who was tossing a cast net into the water, glanced at us, cigarette dangling from his lips. I cringed, wondering what he had heard us say.

"I'm not using magic to help us catch fish," I said at a lower volume. "I can open up my psychic sense, though, so, hopefully, I'll know if a supernatural creature is approaching."

The bail of my spinning reel was open to let the shrimp on my hook drift freely in the current, and suddenly my line spat from the reel.

"I think something's taken your shrimp. Reel it in."

I cranked the handle until I met resistance. My rod jerked and bent like an upside-down U.

"Woo-wee! You've got a fish! Keep your rod pointed up."

My fishing pole throbbed from the underwater fight as I reeled in the line. Occasionally, the reel's drag screamed as the fish gained back line.

Finally, a flopping fish was splashing at the surface of the water below us. Matt leaned over the rail with a long-handled net and scooped up a mangrove snapper.

"Let's put the poor guy back," I said as Matt measured and unhooked the legal-sized fish.

"We have to anger the munuane." Matt said, placing the snapper in a large bucket of seawater and flicking the switch of a battery-operated box clipped to it. "The aerator will keep the fish we catch alive until we're ready to quit. Then, we can release them."

We had arrived at the pier close to midnight, when we assumed it would be deserted. After about an hour, the crowd finally dissipated until we were the only ones there. This was despite the fact that the fish were still biting. We soon had our legal limit of snapper in three buckets.

Matt caught another snapper, and we were officially over our limit. Almost as if on cue, my scalp tingled, and the hair on the back of my head stood up.

"Something is out there," I whispered.

Matt stopped what he was doing and peered into the darkness. Aside from the isolated circles of light on the water from the lamps above, the area between them was pitch black. The massive bridge blocked the sky in front of us, except far to the left and right. Only a red and a green light on bridge pilings next to the channel, far off the end of the pier, pierced the darkness like artificial stars.

A silhouette passed in front of the red light. Did I see a paddling movement?

I touched Matt's arm and pointed, but the shadow had already passed, and the light was visible again.

We stood frozen and listened. There was nothing but a faint breeze and the water lapping against the pilings of the pier. Now and then, a sudden *plunk* of a snook sucking in a baitfish made me jump. The only other sounds were the echoes of tires across the metal grating of the drawbridge out over the channel.

Until the faint splash of a paddle came from just off the end of the pier.

My heart went into my throat, and Matt seized my hand. I quickly went through the steps of a basic protection spell that would contain both of us. Concentrating when panic surges through you is not easy, believe me.

Another splash, even closer this time. It's so much easier to hear sounds over water, and I swore I heard a coarse intake of breath and a low murmur of unintelligible words.

The munuane was coming for us. I was certain of it.

That's why I was confused when a bright light came from behind us. It flooded the entire pier, as well as the water under the bridge in front of us.

The light reflected in a pair of yellow eyes near the surface of the water, only yards away, before they quickly disappeared.

A large splash of someone or something heavy came from where the eyes had disappeared.

Matt and I turned to find the source of the blinding light—a spotlight from a vehicle pulled up at the end of the pier.

A figure silhouetted by the light walked toward us. It was a human.

"How are y'all doing?" asked an aggressive male voice.

"Um, just fine," Matt said.

"Y'all catch any fish?"

The man was close enough now that I could see he was in uniform. As he came right up to us, the paltry ambient light made the patch on his shirt legible: Florida Fish & Wildlife Conservation Commission.

"Yes, sir. We caught a few," Matt said.

"Mind if I look in your buckets?" the officer asked. Without waiting for an answer, he shined a flashlight into each bucket where our catches swam in circles in the oxygenated water.

"Looks like you have one too many snapper, my friends."

"As you can see, we've kept them alive," Matt said. "We were going to release the smallest one."

"That's good to know, but your future intentions don't

matter when it comes to the law. You're over the limit, and I'm afraid I'm going to have to issue a citation."

"Really? For just one fish?" I asked. My fear hadn't gone away enough to give my famous pleading tone enough power.

"Yes. It's for a good cause. The preservation of our fishing stock is important for the economy of Florida and for future generations."

"Yes, sir," Matt and I said in unison as the officer wrote on his pad and tore off the ticket.

He waited while Matt emptied a bucket into the water, releasing the extra fish that just cost us a lot of money, along with all the rest. If the officer was surprised when Matt released them all, he didn't show it.

"Y'all have a good night. Good heavens, it's already past midnight. Drive home safely."

We muttered some inanities and watched him walk back down the pier into the bright light as if he was ascending to heaven. The car drove away, crunching on the gravel of the parking lot.

"It makes me wonder if the munuane works for the FWC," I said.

"I wouldn't be surprised," Matt said as he gathered his gear.

"That was him out there, wasn't it?" I asked in a lower voice.

"Who?"

"Out in the water. Didn't you hear the paddling and see the eyes reflected in the spotlight?"

"Yeah. I thought I was imagining things. Do you think he was coming for us because of the fish?"

"What else would he want?"

Matt was silent. Before he carried the rods, buckets, and tackle bag to the truck, he turned to me.

"To be honest, I didn't believe in the munuane. I thought the murders were committed by humans and were unrelated. Sure, when I got my head bonked on the beach, I couldn't explain it. But only now am I accepting that this aquatic ogre might exist."

"Good. Let's find him and see if he really is a murderer."

CHAPTER 3
PIER PRESSURE

How could I predict where the munuane would strike next? He had appeared twice in the Intra-coastal Waterway. He probably was the one who attacked Matt on the beach. And he even showed up far inland in the northern reaches of the Everglades.

Basically, he could strike anywhere someone was over-fishing or showing cruelty to the denizens of the water. In Florida—with all its shoreline, rivers, lakes, and even tiny retention ponds within housing developments—that could be almost anywhere.

Where would the offenses against water creatures be the worst? Commercial fishing, of course. I'm not making judgments about the industry, but the sheer volume of fish, crabs, lobsters, and other creatures they catch, combined with the brutal inefficiencies of nets and the bycatch they kill, would point toward these fishing boats being the greatest enemies of munuanes.

So, I did some research. It turns out that commercial fishing is a very dangerous line of work. Even in Florida, where the waters aren't as treacherous as Alaska, commercial fishermen have a high rate of accidents and death.

Could any of these actually be murders?

THERE IS no commercial fishing fleet in Jellyfish Beach. It's not like Mayport, in North Florida, where you see flotillas of massive trawlers dragging nets. Instead, you have individual captains in retrofitted recreational fishing boats who catch fish with hook and line, then sell them to seafood markets and restaurants. Then there are the charter boats that take recreational anglers out for half or whole days, ranging from sport-fishing boats to large drift boats that accommodate dozens.

I had seen no news reports of deaths on these boats. But that didn't mean there hadn't been any.

I wasn't sure how to proceed, so I began by asking around at our town's small marina, located off the Intracoastal Waterway only a few miles from the ocean inlet.

Matt and I showed up in the morning, but we were too late to talk to the independent commercial fishermen. They had left before dawn and were out at sea. The crew of a large drift boat, the *Sea Fog*, was getting ready for the first charter of the day. The two young mates loaded bags of ice and boxes of bait while the captain fueled the boat. Matt and I approached him.

"Good morning," I said with a smile.

The captain, a middle-aged man with a deep tan and

wearing a baseball cap that failed to protect his weathered face, smiled back.

"You two want to catch fish? We had a couple of cancellations. You can get tickets in the office over there."

"Thanks, but I'm on the clock," Matt said, flashing his reporter ID. "I'm working on a story and wanted to ask you a few questions."

"I'm kind of busy."

"Keep doing what you're doing. I'll be quick. I was wondering if you or any of the other captains have experienced threats or interference."

The captain, hand on the fuel pump, looked puzzled. "What do you mean?"

"Any violence or vandalism. People giving you a hard time about the fish you caught."

"You mean like environmental crazies? A few showed up to protest once when we returned from a charter. They were bothering the customers while my mates cleaned their fish, so we turned the hoses on them, and they left."

"Have you heard of other boats having problems, here or at sea?" I asked.

He took off his cap and rubbed his bald head.

"Well, Raul Rivas was shot at last week when he was coming in after a day over the reefs. He thought it was just some random idiot playing with a gun."

"Do you think he'll talk with us?" I asked.

"Sure. He runs the Wahoo. Moors it in that slip over there. He should be back in by noon."

We thanked him and wandered through the marina to talk to other captains and boat owners.

"Would a munuane fire a gun?" Matt asked.

"If he can fire a bang stick, why not? Though I admit, Rivas getting shot at sounds pretty random."

We walked from pier to pier, but all the boat slips with signs advertising fishing charters were empty at this time of day. When we came upon a hut advertising a variety of personal-watercraft rentals, I walked in. A skinny young man with bleach-blond dreadlocks and studs in his eyebrows sat on a stool, studying his phone.

"You guys want to rent a couple of PWCs?" he asked.

I asked him the same question we asked the drift boat's captain, even though his customers wouldn't be fishing.

"A group of dudes who rented from us were ticketed for harassing manatees. One of them returned the next day by himself to rent one by himself. He never came back. We found the Jet Ski™ abandoned on Beer Can Island, but no sign of my customer."

"Oh, yes, I remember that case," Matt said. "There was a search for him by water and air, but they never found him. The authorities think a passing boat picked him up and that he just abandoned the Jet Ski, because a body was never found."

After we left the hut, I asked Matt what he thought had happened to the man.

"Personally, I think he's dead. I mean, to rent any kind of personal watercraft, you need to get a temporary safety certificate and leave a large deposit. You're not just going to abandon that money. He probably drowned, and his body was swept out to sea through the inlet. Maybe he was murdered. Who knows, our friend, the munuane, could have done it."

We bought iced teas at the marina concession and waited for Captain Rivas to return.

The boat was a twenty-six-foot center console. Rivas was alone as he piloted the craft from the Intracoastal into the marina, running slowly through the maze of finger piers. He threw out rubber bumpers tied to his boat and drifted into the side of his slip, leaping from the boat like an athlete and tying it off at the bow and stern. He clearly was accustomed to handling his boat all by himself.

"Captain Rivas," Matt said as we approached. "How was the fishing?"

Rivas wore a wide-brimmed hat, held on against the wind with a drawstring, and the typical fishing outfit of nylon shorts and a long-sleeved shirt with venting in the back. He was younger than the captain of the drift boat, but just as weathered. A shiny white scar on his cheek stood out on his tanned face. As he went about securing his vessel, a holster with a handgun was visible on his belt.

He sized us up with suspicion. "I landed a bunch of Mahi. They should fetch a good price."

He wasn't much of a charmer, clearly better suited for commercial fishing than entertaining guests on a charter.

"We're working on a story for *The Jellyfish Beach Journal*," Matt said, "about attacks on fishermen. The captain of the *Sea Fog* said you were shot at recently?"

Rivas nodded. "I was coming in the inlet, and someone took several shots at me." He pointed to the upper part of the hull near the bow. "Two bullet holes."

"Where was the gunfire coming from?"

"Beer Can Island. No one's allowed on that island. I called the Sheriff, and they didn't find anyone there."

Everyone knew Beer Can Island, which sat beside the channel just inside the inlet. It was a spoil island, created by sand dumped after the inlet was dredged. Mangrove trees covered it, and it became a popular spot for boats to pull up to its beach for impromptu parties, hence the name of the island. Eventually, because of the littering and the hazards to navigation created by the congregating boats, the island was closed, with the no-trespassing rule strictly enforced.

It was interesting that the guy who rented the PWC disappeared there.

"I want to search the island," I said.

Matt and Rivas both looked at me like I was crazy.

"No one is allowed there," Rivas said.

"I'm a psychic," I lied, since I couldn't tell him I was a witch. "I want to see if anyone has been living there, or maybe died there, like the guy who rented a Jet Ski from that guy over there and never came back."

"Dead men don't fire weapons," Rivas said.

"No. But the person who killed him could have shot at you. Can you take us to the island?"

"I don't want to get a fine."

"We'll pay you handsomely," Matt said.

"We will?" Since this was Society business, I would be the one who would pay.

"For a thousand, I'll take you there," Rivas said. "If I get fined, it will be at least half of that."

"Well. . ." I ought to talk him down.

"Agreed." Matt said. "In cash."

"I'll take you at night. Less chance of being seen by the Sheriff or Marine Patrol. Meet me here tonight at eleven-thirty."

Like I said before, dealing with supernatural stuff is terrible for your sleep.

When Matt and I parted at our cars to go to our real jobs, I chided him for offering money he didn't have to pay.

"A hunch tells me we really need to explore that island," he explained. "Can your magic help?"

"I can naturally sense if there's a ghost there. And I have spells to tell me if there are any human remains on the island. Or, if there's a supernatural creature around."

"The munuane?"

"Exactly. He could have killed the missing guy and taken shots at Rivas."

"It's not like he's just going to be sitting there, waiting for us to find him."

"I should be able to sense if he was there recently, especially if he left anything behind."

"Like shell casings?"

"Yeah. Or the remains of humans he fed upon."

THE JELLYFISH BEACH MYSTICAL MART AND BOTANICA closes at 10:00 p.m. on Tuesdays. You might wonder why we're open so late. We're not just a hobby shop. For many of the immigrants here in South Florida, a botanica is like a convenience store. When you need a virility potion, you *need* it now. It can't wait until the morning. If a neighbor has put a curse on you, it must be remedied right away. Or, if you need to pray to the likeness of a saint or a god, you'd better do so before you go to bed and the nightmares come.

Also, don't forget the witching hour arrives at midnight. If you're missing certain witchcraft ingredients, you'd better run out and grab them so you can cast your spells at the optimum time.

I watched the clock carefully as closing time approached. The grandfather clock stood in the rear of the store, ticking loudly. Each tick was almost violent, as if a pixie lived inside the clock, striking a hammer.

The clock has been here since Luisa first bought the botanica from an elderly practitioner of obeah, a form of sorcery found in the Caribbean. The obeah man, who has since passed on, said the clock came with the shop when he bought it. No one knows who originally brought it here from the Caribbean. All we know is that we can't let it run down.

I mean that literally. Every morning, whoever opens the shop that day must wind the clock by pulling the chains and lifting the counterweights in front of the pendulum. It takes a few minutes to do.

The legend is that if the clock stops, it will die. And if it dies, unspecified horrible things will happen. The obeah man said if the clock dies, the world will end. Luisa believes that the clock stopping will cause the death of the botanica's owners. Thanks for making me a partner, Luisa!

Older, long-time customers had theories all over the board, such as the stopped clock would unleash a plague or a zombie invasion. All I knew was that it must be wound every day, as if it were a living organism that needed to be fed. Perhaps the six-foot-tall clock—hand-carved from mahogany so dark it was almost black, with a mother-of-pearl clock face, brass hands, and silver inlaid numerals—truly was alive.

The jarring *tick-tick-tick* of the clock reminded me that as soon as it turned ten, I had to lock up, rush home to feed the cats and iguana, then head to the marina to meet Matt and Captain Rivas. Good thing Jellyfish Beach was such a small city that I didn't have to drive far to accomplish this.

I was outside, locking the door, before the deep metallic notes of the clock finished tolling ten. And I parked at the marina at exactly 11:20.

Matt and Rivas were already on the boat, chatting, when I hurried down the pier. Matt offered me a hand as I stepped down onto the deck.

"Captain Rivas was telling me funny stories about his hometown in Venezuela," he said.

"I came from a small, poor village in the south of the country," the captain said. "But it was a happy place to grow up. All my relatives have come to the States now because of the dictator."

"I'd love to hear the stories sometime," I said.

"My pleasure. But tonight, we must be silent, so if anyone is on the island, we can surprise them. And so we don't alert law enforcement."

After moving through the marina at idle speed, Rivas gunned the motor, and we cruised up the Intracoastal with the boat rising on plane. Immediately after crossing the channel inside the inlet, he pulled back on the throttle, and the boat settled down. We chugged forward at minimal speed, and Rivas turned off the running lights. Soon, we were far enough away from the lights of the inlet and its public park that we moved through deep darkness with only the light of the half moon and Rivas's sharp vision to guide us.

A dark mass was ahead of us: Beer Can Island. As we got closer, I could distinguish the dark green of the mangroves. Then, a narrow strip of white—the beach—was visible.

Rivas cut the engine and quietly slid an anchor into the water, stopping the boat about fifty yards from the beach.

"We are in shallow water here," Rivas whispered. "We will wade to the island from here so my boat won't be seen near the island."

Fortunately, I was wearing sneakers. Rivas dropped a dive ladder from the stern, and we climbed into the water, Matt, me, then Rivas. The water was thigh-deep, not too cold, and the bottom was firm sand.

The narrow beach was a steep incline, and we had to grab the branches of a mangrove to pull ourselves onto flat ground. The wide beach where boats used to pull up was on the opposite side of the small island, visible to homes along the shore of the Intracoastal. This side was much more private. We entered the trees and waited silently, listening.

The only sound was the wind rustling the mangrove leaves.

All my senses were open, including my sixth sense, searching for signs of anything living or dead. Aside from birds, lizards, insects, and fish, nothing was here. No humans, for certain.

I cast a spell that reacted to supernatural energy. Yes, there was some here. No living supernatural entity was on the island now, but one or more had been here recently, leaving traces of their energy.

And a spirit? Yes, I sensed a haunting. The ghost of a human was around, but not currently manifesting itself. I assumed the human had died here, but I couldn't tell how long ago or if it was male or female.

We passed into a clearing. The remains of a campfire were in the center. Ashes were visible, so there had been a fire after the most recent rain. It could be from people who had snuck onto the island like us.

"Did the munuane do this?" Matt whispered the other possibility.

Rivas knelt beside the ashes and looked at Matt with surprise.

My spell alerted me to the nearby evidence of a supernatural creature. So did my nose. I used a stick to push sand away from a hole at the edge of the clearing.

"What's in there?" Matt asked.

Rivas shushed him.

I easily recognized what it was, and my spell told me with certainty that it came from a supernatural creature, in particular, one from the ogre family.

"Poop," I said. "Ogre poop."

"Are you serious?" Matt asked.

"Yes, Matt. Even monsters need to poop."

"I know about munuanes," Rivas said. "We had them in Venezuela. And there must be one here in Florida."

I caught Matt's eyes in the moonlight, and he nodded.

It was time for me to ask the Friends of Cryptids Society to send in the cavalry.

CHAPTER 4
A SEA CHANGE

When I became Luisa's partner, I thought I had left nursing behind. But nursing is a calling, not just a profession. Caring for people is in my blood as fundamentally as magic is. Many of my home-health patients wanted to continue seeing me after I "retired" from nursing, even though the nursing agency that catered to supernaturals offered them suitable substitutes. One thing about me, I have a hard time saying no.

So, there I was, bright and early on a Thursday morning, walking down the seventh-floor breezeway of Seaweed Manor's Building A. Next door to the vampire community in Squid Tower, Seaweed Manor was home to aging werewolves. Werewolves don't live forever like vampires, so the population here was in constant flux.

Normal humans lived here, too, along with the werewolves and a few other supernatural beings. The humans were, shall we say, the types who preferred to keep a low profile. They were highly unlikely to call the police if they saw unusual activity, such as wolves surfing beneath the full moon.

Seaweed Manor was the only condo community on the beach around here that was remotely affordable. When you saw the condition of the property, you would assume the HOA fees were low.

Harry and Cindy Roarke's condo was well kept and had been recently renovated. While I measured their blood pressure and oxygen levels at their dining-room table, I complimented them on their new kitchen.

"The demo was the best part," Harry said. "We shifted to wolf and tore the old kitchen apart in a frenzy of destruction."

"It was like therapy," said Cindy, who dressed like a hippie.

I asked Harry, the HOA president, if the werewolves were still feuding with the vampires.

"No, but those snobs still complain about our landscaping. And whenever they find litter, they blame us, even though it's obvious it comes from cars driving by on A1A."

"I'm glad you don't allow the disagreements to escalate," I said.

"I'm glad you don't spend as much time at Squid Tower anymore," Cindy said, patting my arm. "There were times we were afraid you were going to be turned."

"They would never turn me. They appreciate my services." I didn't mention Mrs. Steinhauer's involuntary attack on me that finally convinced me to give up nursing full time.

"We were afraid you'd want to be turned," Harry said. He smiled through his bushy beard, but his eyes were serious. "That you wanted to be one of them."

"I wouldn't want to be a vampire. I don't mind getting old and dying."

I was a bit taken aback to hear the Roarkes thought that way about me. In truth, I felt the pangs of loneliness that came from not having a family. Never having remarried after my divorce, I didn't have children. My adoptive parents moved to Tennessee, and though my father passed away not long after, I tried to see my mother at least twice a year. My birth mother, who I had grown up believing was deceased, was actually alive. The problem was, she was an evil black-magic sorceress who had tried to kill me twice and appeared to be involved in recent black-magic incidents in Jellyfish Beach.

All I had were my pets and my friends. That's why the vampires at Squid Tower became my surrogate family. They were like parents and grandparents who would never die. The Roarkes were family to me, too. I guess that explains why I still had home-health patients, even though the botanica and the Friends of Cryptids Society kept me so busy.

Speaking of which, I asked the Roarkes if they were aware of a new supernatural creature in the area. Supernaturals are very territorial and have a good sense of when others are in the vicinity.

"Supernaturals are always moving to Florida," Harry said. "They used to come from the Northeast, just like the humans, but now, they come from everywhere. They're ruining Florida."

Cindy nodded in agreement. "Clogging the roads and driving up real-estate prices."

"You mean humans or supernaturals?"

"Both."

"And really, how many vampires can a community sustain before it becomes unlivable? Literally," Harry added.

"What about ogres?" I asked.

"Personally, I don't care for them," Cindy said.

"I mean, do you know of new ogres showing up in Jellyfish Beach? There are reports of a South American ogre called the munuane, which has been attacking fishermen."

Both Roarkes shook their heads in the negative.

"We'll keep our noses open for unfamiliar scents and we'll ask around," Harry said.

I was certain at least one munuane was here, especially after finding the poop on Beer Can Island, but I needed any information I could get. I explained this.

"Now, you've got us intrigued," Cindy said. "We'll shift tonight and see if we can pick up a trail."

After the health screenings, I walked to the end of the community's wooden dune crossover and sat on a bench overlooking the ocean. I love the beach, but rarely have the time to hang out on it. It was times like this when I wished I had a beachfront condo, though the cost and maintenance would be so steep. Being a nurse and running a botanica are not the pathways to riches, let me tell you.

The wind was from the west this morning, and the ocean was smooth. There was barely any surf. A woman wearing a bikini lazily paddled southward on her paddle board. A freighter chugged by, far out near the horizon. In between were several sport-fishing boats of various sizes.

I recognized the *Sea Fog* drifting over the reefs that were only a few hundred yards from shore. The seventy-foot vessel was packed with fishermen lined along the rails. The sky was cloudless, and the water shimmered in the sun. It was a perfect day to be in Florida.

I saw the burst of flames and smoke a second before I heard the explosion. The *Sea Fog* rocked violently as debris sailed into the air and landed on the water like hail. A handful of the fishermen had fallen into the water.

It took a moment for my brain to register that there had been an explosion on board. I jumped off the bench and ran down the stairs to the beach, calling 911. The operator said they'd already received several calls. When I reached the edge of the surf, I stopped. What did I think I was going to do? The boat was too far out for me to reach it by swimming, and even though I was a nurse, there was little I could do to help.

But I had magic. I'd never needed to help explosion victims before, but there was no time to waste in learning how.

The first thing I did was focus on the people in the water. Life preservers were already being tossed from the *Sea Fog* to the victims in the water. But I saw one person, her head barely above the surface, who might be unconscious. I improvised a spell that created buoyancy, making the water around the victim denser and pushing her body upward to keep her head above the surface.

I want to dispel any ideas you may have that a witch like me has the power to levitate someone hundreds of yards away out of the water. If they were nearby, maybe I could do it. But not way out there. My spell was working though—her head protruded from the water as if she were wearing a life vest. Someone swam up to her and pulled her toward a life raft that had dropped nearby.

With my next spell, I attempted to extinguish the fire

onboard. Again, the boat's distance from me made it difficult for my magic to reach it. Somehow, I pinpointed the core of the fire and constructed a spell that sucked the oxygen away from it. Soon, the dark smoke rising from the boat thinned out, and I could no longer see flames.

By now, rescue boats were arriving on the scene. The deep drumming of a helicopter filled the air as the Coast Guard aircraft soared over me out to the *Sea Fog*. It hovered over the boat, lowering a metal stretcher to the ocean's surface. A diver splashed down and pulled a floating passenger onto the stretcher.

There was nothing else I could do to help the people on the boat. They were in expert hands now.

Breaking my focus on the spells, I realized I'd been joined by numerous people standing at the edge of the weak surf, capturing images of the scene with their phones. I pulled out my phone, only to discover several texts from Matt. He'd heard about the explosion on his police scanner and realized it was offshore of where my clients lived. He wondered if I was there. I texted my late reply.

Yes, I'm here. I saw it happen.

Is it true there are casualties? he asked.

Yes. I don't know how many.

Is the ship in danger of sinking?

I don't think so.

Do you think the munuane did this?

I paused while I thought about it. My first instinct was to say yes, though it would depend on what caused the explosion. If it turned out to be a bomb, then no, I didn't think the ogre did it. But possibly the creature monkeyed with the engine and fuel lines. Or maybe he used magic.

Too early to say, I replied. *Can you get surveillance footage from the marina?*

Doubt it. The police probably already have it, and they won't share.

I had to get away from the crowd and the distressing sight of the *Sea Fog*. Driving didn't seem like a good idea in my state of mind, so I walked north along the beach toward the inlet. The tide was going out, leaving good sand for walking: slightly damp and firm.

Soon, the crowd was far behind me. Several beachfront mansions had been built on this stretch of shoreline. They were excessively large, with overly extravagant architecture, making them the perfect target for my populist resentment. The good thing about these billionaires' homes was the beach was usually empty behind them. This morning, there were no people at all ahead of me.

Which was why the footprints grabbed my eyes. Fresh footprints led from the ocean onto the beach, the only ones in view.

And they weren't human.

The prints were made by feet that were vaguely human-like. They had heels and toes similar to ours, but the feet were massive. The prints sank deep into the sand, indicating enormous weight. They were wide at the toes and showed signs of long claws protruding from the nails.

They were the footprints of a monster. Specifically, I would guess, an ogre.

Did the munuane land here after swimming from the *Sea Fog*?

CHAPTER 5

PRESS CONFERENCE GOES THONG

The first time I met Mrs. Lupis and Mr. Lopez, they had given me their business cards. Each crisp white card held only a name and a phone number. There was no logo and not even the name of the Society. And for names, "Lupis" and "Lopez" were all that was printed. No first names or work titles.

The phone numbers on the cards were identical. Aside from texting Mrs. Lupis at a different number once, this would be my first time calling this number. My two handlers usually simply showed up out of the blue when needed.

The phone rang twice before it was answered by a recording.

"Thank you for calling. To report a sighting, press 1. To report an attack, press 2. To make a donation and receive a free tote bag and wall calendar, press 3. For Wordle clues, press 4. For all other inquiries, or to speak with an agent, please stay on the line."

Music began, bubblegum pop from the 1960s.

The Friends of Cryptids Society of the Americas just got weirder and weirder the more I dealt with them.

I was on hold for a while and grew impatient, so I went into the kitchen, filled the kettle, and put it on the stove. As the water simmered, my doorbell rang. I sighed and headed to the front door.

It was Mrs. Lupis and Mr. Lopez.

"Hey, I was just trying to call you."

"We know," they said in unison.

"Um, how?"

"It's our job to know things," Mr. Lopez said.

"Life is so much more efficient that way," Mrs. Lupis added.

I let them in and offered tea, which they declined. They sat at my kitchen table while I prepared my cup. Kind of déjà vu from the other day.

"We assume you contacted us because you have documented evidence of the munuane?" Mrs. Lupis asked.

"Um, no. I haven't even seen him, though I came close a few times."

"Can you be more specific?" Mr. Lopez asked.

"I heard him and saw his eyes in the darkness one night."

They stared at me, unimpressed.

"I found some of his stool."

"Did you take a sample?" Mr. Lopez asked.

"No! Gross."

"This is a matter of science," Mrs. Lupis admonished.

"Okay. And I found what I believe were his footprints."

"Did you make a plaster mold?" Mr. Lopez asked.

I shook my head, getting annoyed.

"Did you take a photo?"

"Yes. That, I did."

I pulled it up on my phone. And passed it to them.

"I put a pen beside the prints to give a sense of scale."

The two passed the phone back and forth, grunting each time they looked at the photo.

"Definitely from the ogre family," Mrs. Lupis said.

"I agree. It's not at all troll-like," Mr. Lopez offered.

"The reason I contacted you is that I do believe now that the munuane has been murdering humans."

The two looked at me without a trace of surprise.

I summarized the attacks on the snapper fisherman, the alligator hunters, the missing man whose Jet Ski was found off Beer Can Island, and the *Sea Fog*. I mentioned its attack on Matt, too.

"But you have no proof that the munuane was responsible?" Mr. Lopez asked.

"Well, I detected some supernatural energy. Like the poop. The poop positively reeked of the supernatural. Sorry, bad wording."

"So far, the footprint is the only evidence we actually have," Mrs. Lupis said. "And it only shows the munuane was on the beach around the time the fishing boat was attacked. It doesn't prove the beast carried out the attack."

I shrugged. "Look, I've done the best I can. I think it's time to bring in your enforcer before more humans die."

"If Angela finds the munuane, she can interrogate it," Mrs. Lupis said to her partner. "There's no need for her to put it down unless we're certain it killed the humans."

"Perhaps you're right. Miss Mindle here seems incapable of making contact with it."

His tone rankled me, but I ignored my feelings. "I'll show her where I found the poop. I think the munuane spends time there."

The two rose from their chairs. "She will get in touch with you," Mr. Lopez said as they left.

I could just go to the Jellyfish Beach Public Library and speak with her, but I had to respect the proper protocol and wait for her to reach out to me.

The more I worked with the Friends of Cryptids Society, the less sense they made to me.

I WATCHED the local news coverage of the *Sea Fog* incident, which they were calling a bombing. The anchor and reporters of Channel Five in Mullet City were almost giddy at the momentousness of it for Crab County and tiny Jellyfish Beach. We had boat fires now and then, but never an explosion that appeared to be from a bomb. Could this be terrorism? The on-air team seemed to think it was. You could imagine them calculating the boost to their ratings.

They cut to a press conference with Jellyfish Beach's new chief of police. He had recently replaced an interim chief who had filled in after our long-serving chief retired. The new guy, Chief Dullart, apparently wanted to have the smoldering *Sea Fog* as his backdrop before it was towed back to the marina.

It wasn't such a good idea to have the conference on the beach, though. The wind had picked up since this morning, and it made his hairpiece twitch like it was trying to escape. Also, the wind played havoc with the audio as it buffeted the microphone.

You need to give us a break here in Crab County. We're a small market and not quite ready for prime time. In this era of ubiquitous video, everyone tries to act like they're in the major leagues, but we're more like a bunch of kids playing ball in someone's backyard.

Chief Dullart, flanked by two senior officers, droned on about the explosion. One passenger was killed, and fifteen were injured.

"What caused the explosion?" a reporter shouted.

"I'll get to that," the chief snapped. "I haven't opened this up to questions yet."

He said the explosion wasn't caused by a mechanical mishap; it was most likely from a device or external cause. The FBI would help identify the explosive.

"We believe this incidence is connected to three recent murders."

Of course, I believed that was the case, but I was surprised the police linked three very different types of violence.

"A recreational fisherman was drowned at the causeway, and his death was ruled a homicide. In addition, two alligator hunters were murdered in the Wikowackee National Wildlife Preserve west of Jellyfish Beach. Investigators believe all these incidents are connected."

An overweight man, wearing a bathing suit that was little more than a thong, wandered into the background of the shot, oblivious to the cameras pointing his way. He turned to stare at the ocean, giving viewers at home the unwanted view of the butt cheeks his skimpy swimwear didn't cover.

The chief, unaware of the distraction behind him, continued his earnest stare at the cameras.

"Based on evidence collected at the crime scenes, and outstanding detective work by our department, I can confidently declare that the motive for the killings was eco-terrorism."

The crowd of reporters gasped. I wasn't sure if it was in response to the chief's assertion, or the fact the fat guy behind him was doing squats on the sand. It was a disturbing sight.

"There are several local environmental activists who are persons of interest in this case. I'll now open it up to questions."

"Chief Dullart, do you think you'll *crack* this case?" The voice of the reporter was Matt's.

A few snickers came from the crowd.

The chief's subordinates glowered at the cameras, unaware of the spectacle going on behind them, so they couldn't clear the scene or warn the chief.

"I believe we will," the chief said. "We have a good team."

"When will you get to the *bottom* of this?" asked another reporter.

"Soon. We've begun interviewing persons of interest."

"Do you know which environmental group is *behind* these murders?" Matt asked.

"I cannot release that information at this time."

It looked like the reporters would run out of buttocks double-entendres, and the chief could end the conference with most of his dignity intact.

But the wind picked up. And so did his toupee. It flopped around on his head like those scary inflatable men outside of car dealerships.

Fortunately for him, one of his officers must have realized something was up by the expressions on the crowd's faces. He turned to his boss, saw the toupee about to leap for freedom, and whispered in the chief's ear.

The chief angrily slammed his uniform cap upon his skull and announced the press conference was over. His face was the darkest shade of purple I'd ever seen on a human, and I was worried about him having a cardiovascular event.

Secretly, I hoped the chief was right about humans committing the murders. If the ogre was guilty, my life would be a nightmare. If humans were the culprits, the justice machine's gears would grind along, and I wouldn't lose any sleep.

On second thought, I would probably lose sleep, anyway.

CHAPTER 6
MAGIC AND MEMORY

"I penned something different," Walt Whitman announced to my vampire creative-writing group. "The gentlemen of the group," he nodded toward Sol, Martin, and Schwartz, "seem to enjoy action and adventure."

The male vampires smiled, baring their fangs in a macho display.

"Therefore, I present this sketch based on my experience in the American Civil War." The famous poet, and not-so-famous psychic vampire, cleared his throat as he unfolded a paper manuscript.

"Elmer McFadden, a callow youth from Delaware, lay in the cot, wrapped in bandages up to his neck," Walt read in a tender voice. "Of him I asked what I could do to salve his pain? In a faint whisper, he asked me to play 'Jeanie with the Light Brown Hair' with his harmonica. He said it reminded him of his home and his sweetheart.

"'I cannot play the harmonica,' I said with sadness. 'But I can hum the tune for you.'

"Elmer smiled weakly. I took that as an acceptance of my offer. Thus, I hummed the popular song that the youth grasped at to draw himself back to his happier past, like a man who fell into a raging sea tugging, pulling on a rope to heave himself back to safety.

"Oh, Elmer, I thought as I hummed the tune—and the patients in nearby beds glared at me angrily—you have idealized the past. You have forgotten all the sadness you had borne and remember only the moments of youthful joy. But in this time of suffering from your wounds, at the brink of your life expiring, you may be forgiven for gilding your memories. For now, you need the distant beacon of innocence to shine brighter. You need—"

"Excuse me," Martin interrupted. "Are you trying to put us to sleep again? I'd prefer not to have my psychic energy drained, thank you."

"I thought this was supposed to be a war story," Sol complained. "I thought you fought in the war."

"I served as a nurse in army hospitals," Walt said, chagrined.

"A nurse?"

"What's wrong with being a nurse?" I asked.

"Nothing," Sol said. "I was hoping to hear about a bayonet charge at Antietam or something exciting like that."

"With blood spilled," Martin added.

"Yeah. Gunfire and lots of blood."

"I'm sorry I have disappointed you, gentlemen."

"Can I read from my story now?" Gladys asked. "It's about a lonely vampire who—"

"Seduces the pool boy," Schwartz said. "Heard it a thousand times already."

"Actually, in this one, she seduces the mail carrier."

I settled down for another of Gladys's saucy romances, when Agnes caught my eye from the doorway. I leaped from my seat to see what she wanted, happy for the excuse to avoid hearing the love scene.

"I didn't mean to interrupt you," Agnes said. "After your class is over, can you consult with a resident who needs medical advice?"

"Sure," I said. "How about if I do it now?"

"I don't want you to end the class early."

I wanted to end it early, but I didn't want to hurt any feelings. I returned to the circle of chairs.

Gladys was still reading. "'I bring you a special delivery,' the strapping mail carrier said. 'I didn't want to shove it into your mailbox without the special attention you deserve.'"

I groaned silently as Gladys went on, and tried not to grimace like the men in the group.

IN THE CARD room across the hall, Agnes sat at a table with a couple who appeared to be in their eighties in body age. The husband, who had a full head of white hair, looked up expectantly. The wife, a mousy woman with short hair dyed brown, smiled at me. I instantly noticed the slight confusion in her eyes.

"Missy Mindle, I'd like you to meet Philip and Dorita Pound."

I shook their cold-as-death hands and sat down. "What can I do for you?"

"Dorita struggles with dementia," Philip said. "She has an early stage, and since she was turned into a vampire, it hasn't progressed. Thankfully. But when she's having a bad day, I wish there were more I could do."

"I take those supplements they advertise on TV that are supposed to sharpen your mind," Dorita said. "They don't work. Is it because I'm a vampire?"

"No, it's because they don't work. As you know, medical science does not have a cure for Alzheimer's or other forms of dementia," I said. "There have been new prescription medications that slow its progression. But you, obviously, wouldn't need those."

"I told them you're also a witch," Agnes said. "Perhaps magic could help a bit."

My life's ambition was to use magic to help people. Nothing makes me happier than when my magic heals patients more effectively than medical care alone.

As we all know, vampires have preternatural healing abilities, but these mostly help with wounds and injuries. Age-based maladies they had prior to being turned often don't go away when they become vampires. Sure, their arthritic knees and hips can move a lot faster, but the underlying disease isn't cured, only halted in its progression.

The problem with using my magic for healing is that patients expect miracles. But magic isn't like that. It must work within the physiological constraints of a patient. It can bend, but not break, the scientific laws of the earth.

I tried to explain this as gently as I could.

"Sometimes—not always—my magic can ease symptoms temporarily," I said. "But only temporarily. It can ease the pain of a toothache, for example, but not fix the cavity causing it."

It could pull the tooth, but I didn't want to mention that.

"We just want a little help when she's having a difficult day," Philip said.

"You told me once you have a recollection spell," Agnes said.

"Yes." I had used the spell recently on a witness to the church defilements. "That's what I have in mind for Mrs. Pound. We can try it tonight if you want."

"Yes, please," Dorita said.

"Now, it would be impractical for you to rely on me to come by and cast the spell every time you have a difficult day. But if this works, I can transfer the magic into a potion you can drink."

"Thank you so much," Philip said with a big smile, though he still had sadness in his eyes.

"We were both turned on the same night," Dorita said.

"Yes. We were leaving a restaurant, and a young thug accosted us outside. Turns out he was a vampire, too lazy to prey on younger people. Dorita looked like an easy meal to him. He took her right there. I punched and kicked him—did everything I could to stop him, but he was too strong. There was nothing nearby I could use as a stake. So, I was forced to watch him drain her to death. I sobbed, and the thug took pity on me. He offered to turn her, and I said only if he turned me, too. The thug complained he was too full from his meal, but I insisted. And that's how we could stay together for eternity."

They both smiled, but there was a tinge of sadness in their eyes. They were together, but sometimes Dorita wasn't fully there. I leaned over and placed my hand on hers.

"I'll do my best."

I had learned and practiced my recollection spell well enough that I didn't need to be within a magic circle to cast it. I couldn't afford that luxury when I needed help with my or someone else's memory.

So, I simply cleared my mind and slowed my breathing and heart rate. With all my concentration, I pictured the core of my energies deep inside me. I willed it to grow larger and stronger, absorbing all the energies within me and drawing upon the elemental energies of the earth around me.

I took Dorita's hands in mine and chanted the words quietly, a mixture of Latin and Old English.

When I said the last word, the energy rose from my solar plexus, flowed through my arms, and into Dorita's hands. Her body twitched as it received the magic via the energy.

Her eyes opened wide. They were bright and intense.

"What is the name of our community?" Philip asked her.

"Why, Squid Tower, of course."

"What street is it on?"

"A1A."

"What did you have for dinner last night?"

"Type O-positive. It was delicious."

"Good, good. What street was our first house on?"

"Alexander Avenue."

"Where did you go to college?"

"Um. . ." She struggled. "Harvard?"

"No, that's where I went. Keep trying."

"It's right there on the edge of my mind," she said, frustrated.

Philip glanced at me with concern.

"It starts with a V," he said.

"Vassar! Yes, Vassar."

"Good."

"You don't want to push her too hard," I advised.

"What was our son's nickname?"

Her eyes no longer burned. They clouded over as if she were shutting down. Her son might not be alive; vampire parents outlive their human children. The emotion of loss could easily derail her cognition.

She struggled to say a word, as if she had a speech impediment. Finally, she slumped in defeat.

"I can't. I can't remember."

"It's okay," Philip said, hugging her. "It was Little Man."

"I'm sorry," I said. "My spell wore off too quickly or wasn't strong enough."

Philip continued to hold his wife, a tear inching down his cheek. It looked like he was bleeding, which is why you don't want to make vampires cry. I felt horrible.

"I'll work on another spell. A stronger one that's more targeted to Dorita's condition."

"It's okay," Philip said. "It is what it is."

"I promise I'll try to do better."

'Please, we have no right to ask you to go through all this trouble."

My drive to heal was only strengthened by this failure. There was no stopping me now.

"I apologize for putting you in an awkward position," Agnes said as she walked me out to my car.

"Don't apologize. I'll develop a better spell if it's the last thing I do. You'll hear from me when I have one."

IT WAS A BIG CUBAN WEDDING, and the church was packed. Though this would be Luisa's brother's second marriage, it was the bride's first, and she had insisted on all the trappings. I sat with Luisa and her two daughters through a preliminary mass that seemed endless.

And, in case you're wondering, being a Santeria priestess didn't interfere at all with Luisa's Christian faith. In fact, they sort of enhanced each other. In Luisa's eyes, the more religions you practice, the better. They give meaning to our lives, so why not go to the all-you-can-eat buffet?

Try as I may, I couldn't relax and enjoy the ceremony. I had black magic on my mind.

A series of incidents had occurred recently in the various houses of worship of Jellyfish Beach. At first, they seemed like tasteless pranks, such as leaving cow dung in front of the buildings. But they progressed, becoming dangerous and sinister.

Black-magic altars were found outside the front doors. These were occult tableaux with piles of human bones, bowls of blood, black candles, and other creepy items. My ghost roommate, Don Mateo, informed me of their purpose.

It was to steal the soul of anyone who left the house of worship and passed by the evil altar. The victim's soul would remain behind in the house of worship. The victim, missing their soul, would soon perish. Or, even worse, become possessed by something evil.

Worst of all, I was convinced my mother was behind this. The black-magic sorceress was back to her evil ways. But with all the opportunities for evil in the state of Florida, why did she have to be doing it in my town?

As far as I knew, no one had lost their soul yet, because I had spread the word through Detective Cindy Shortle to all the congregations to be on the lookout for these altars and remove them immediately.

And today, as the priest droned on, my senses were heightened. I had set magical wards outside the church to warn me of any evil activity, and I was totally not paying attention to the service. Sorry. At least I could blame it on the wards.

The organ began playing a hymn as the wedding couple received communion, continuing as the rest of the congregation lined up to receive theirs. I glanced at my watch. We hadn't even gotten to the actual wedding ceremony yet.

I was formulating a joke to whisper to Matt, who sat beside me opposite Luisa, when my scalp began prickling and my palms perspired. I switched my brain to Magic Mode.

Yep, the wards I had set outside were raising an alarm. Images flickered in my brain of a green imp squatting on the church steps. He was setting up a black-magic altar.

When first entering the church, I had noticed a security camera above the front doors. I was certain that the video it was shooting would show the bones and blood, but not the imp. Cameras almost always fail to capture supernatural creatures. Don't ask me why.

When it was our row's turn to head toward the altar for our communion wafers, I headed in the opposite direction. Not because I'm a sinner, but because I wanted to destroy the black-magic altar before anyone got hurt. I strode quickly down the aisle, ignoring the curious or judgmental gazes of the people I passed.

I was only twenty feet from the door when a cellphone went off. It was the theme song of *The Flintstones* from the '60s. Now, everyone was glaring at the man who didn't silence his phone instead of at me.

He squeezed out of the row and darted to the door to take his call outside.

"Wait!" I called.

Too late. He opened the door and slipped out. I hurried after him, grabbing the door handle before the door swung closed behind him.

When I stepped out onto the portico, the sight shocked me. Shortle had shown me a photo of one of these black-magic altars, but seeing one in person touched some primitive part of my brain, causing intense fear and distress. It must have been the sight of all the blood in the bowl, the way the human bones were arrayed, the sulfurous scent of the candles, the nauseating reek of the herbs and powders sprinkled everywhere.

My witchy senses went haywire from the cloud of evil energy hanging over the church's entrance.

I was too late. The man I had tried to stop was halfway down the walkway to the parking lot, shouting at his phone. He was one of those people who mysteriously prefers to use his phone on speaker mode all the time.

If he had lost his soul, he wasn't showing it yet.

I carefully picked up the bowl of blood and placed it on the ground behind a large philodendron beside the steps. A crime-scene technician could do what he or she pleased with it. As for the rest of the tableau, I kicked it off the steps, releasing my pent-up anger. I wanted no congregant to see it or suffer its evil effects.

The man still spoke loudly into his phone, unaware that he had lost his soul. Had it been replaced already by something else?

I wondered if I should go check on him. Could my nursing skills detect if he was missing his soul? He kept shouting into his phone—something about a hedge fund.

Maybe, I hoped, the spell hadn't worked, and he still had his soul.

But, as I opened the door to go back inside, my magical senses heard and felt a swoosh of something rocketing from the church entrance up into the sky.

It was a soul; I was certain of it.

I prayed it was on its way to Heaven, and not feeding a hungry demonic force.

The wedding, by the way, turned out to be lovely. And the reception was wild. There was no black magic in the entire world strong enough to put a damper on a Cuban-American wedding.

"Did you notice that guy whose phone rang during communion?" I asked Luisa at the reception. He never came back into the church, and I had seen no sign of him when we all left the church.

"Yeah. Dave. He's the husband of a distant cousin."

"He exited the church and walked right through a black-magic altar. I think his soul was taken from him."

"He's a hedge-fund manager. I don't think he has a soul."

"I'm serious. Do you know if he's okay? He's probably been possessed by another entity."

"I'll ask around about him." Luisa laughed as she watched a group of relatives dancing. She was not taking this seriously.

Neither did Matt when I told him about the altar and the imp. He said I shouldn't get involved because I was already too over-my-head in supernatural affairs.

But I believed my mother was behind this black-magic plot. Which meant I felt duty-bound to stop it.

The Friends of Cryptids Society was not concerned, either, when I texted them about it. They said sorcery was not their purview. They would appreciate it, however, if I could get a photo of the imp.

No one would take it seriously. I had badgered Luisa to check with her distant cousin to see if Dave was okay. She was never able to reach her cousin.

There was nothing more I could do.

CHAPTER 7
OGRE ISLAND

It used to be when my doorbell rang, it would either be a delivery or a solicitation.

"The tree in your front yard seriously needs trimming. And we're offering a special price."

Or:

"Your driveway needs sealing. And we're offering a special price."

Or:

"Do you mind if I pick some of your mangoes?"

Or quite often:

"Can we leave you with these pamphlets about Jesus?"

Or too frequently:

"Hi, I'm a runaway, being held hostage by bad people. I need to sell magazine subscriptions to earn my food."

Or most frequently:

"Hi, my soccer team needs to earn money for uniforms and to pay our coach's alimony. Can you buy these raffle tickets?"

Now, however, I was just as likely to find Mr. Lopez and Mrs. Lupis standing at my front door. Today, when the doorbell rang just as I was about to get into the shower, I was surprised that it was the Society's enforcer, Angela Davie.

"Sorry to bother you," said the diminutive, grandmotherly librarian.

"Not at all, Angela. Please come in. Would you like some tea?"

"Oh, no, please don't trouble yourself. I'm here to speak to you about the munuane. Do you have a moment?"

I realized my shower would be delayed, as well as my arrival at the botanica.

"Sure, no problem." We sat in the living room, and I texted Luisa that I would be late.

"Mrs. Lupis and Mr. Lopez were disappointed I hadn't encountered the munuane directly," I said. "That's why they sent you."

"No offense, but as a mage, my magic is generally more powerful than yours. They wanted to see if I'd have better luck in finding the creature."

"I'm not offended. I'm relieved all the burden isn't entirely on me. Did you hear, though, the police suspect eco-terrorists?"

She flipped her hand dismissively. "That bald bonehead of a chief doesn't know how to tie his own shoes. Blaming the deaths on some far-fetched conspiracy makes him look less incompetent when he can't solve the cases."

"So, you think the munuane *is* the killer?"

"I'm not jumping to any conclusions until we find the answer. If he is the killer, I'll have to deal with him."

"By putting him down?"

"Not necessarily. I'll give him the option to move back to South America. I don't take killing monsters lightly because some species are on the decline. Except for vampires and were-wolves, of course. There are too many of them."

"I can show you the places where we believe we encoun-tered the munuane," I said. "The place I want to show you first is a spoil island just inside of the inlet. My magic told me a supernatural creature had been there, and he even left droppings."

"Did you take samples?" She looked at me sternly. With bifocals perched on her nose and her white hair in a bun, she was the archetypical librarian who scolds you for talking.

"You're the second person who asked me. No, I did not take samples of the monster poop, though I really wish I had."

"When can you take me?"

"Tonight. We can't be seen trespassing on the island. Bring your canoe. It will be safer to paddle there than to take a boat. Also, I don't have a boat."

WE MET at 11:00 pm at the inlet park, where we launched on the sandy beach of a cove on the Intracoastal. I paddled my kayak, and Angela followed in her canoe. She was a strong paddler for someone her age, though she might have enhanced her strength with magic.

The water was choppy, making the paddling difficult. As we approached the island, a nearly full moon glittered off the tips of the waves and the leaves of the dark green mangroves at the water's edge. The mound shape rising above the water had a sense of malevolence tonight.

I cast a protection spell around myself. Angela, more powerful magically than I, could protect herself.

My spell that detects supernatural energy was bothering my mind like a small child tugging at my shirtsleeve. That meant there was a good chance the munuane—or an entirely different monster—was on the island tonight.

Angela maneuvered her canoe beside me.

"Do you sense what I'm feeling?" she asked.

"Yes. Something is on the island. Here's a plan: I'll approach it from the east side, like most people do, and land on the beach. You come from this side facing the main channel. The mangroves look impenetrable, but there's a path through them we used before. When I land, I'll make a lot of noise, and, hopefully, that will drive the creature toward you."

Normally, I wouldn't want to put someone else in harm's way, but Angela was the enforcer. She was here tonight to make contact with the munuane and would be prepared if things got hairy.

After we crossed the inlet's channel that bisected the waterway's main channel to our left, I turned away from Angela and paddled to the right of the island.

Leaving Angela behind me, my ears popped slightly as I left her magical field. I hadn't even realized I was in it before, and now I felt more vulnerable.

The waters were calm between the island and the west shore of the strip of land that held Highway A1A and the ocean beaches. I was out of the wind here. This side of the island had shallow water and a picturesque crescent beach, shining white in the moonlight at the edge of the dark trees. I paddled quickly toward it until my kayak slid onto the sand, coming to a halt. My paddle rattled against the plastic hull as I climbed out. I dropped the paddle on the kayak to make even more noise.

Making sure my protection spell was extended, I walked across the beach and into the trees.

Something crunched through the underbrush in the darkness ahead of me. The bit of moonlight leaking through the trees caught a dark, looming shadow moving away from me.

"I mean you no harm," I said, not entirely truthfully.

My spell for detecting supernatural energy was going haywire. And I smelled the creature: a rank, musk-like scent. Thank goodness it was moving away from me.

Which meant it was moving toward Angela. I didn't know if she had landed yet. Then, her voice came across the water, just offshore of the island.

"Greetings, munuane. I am Angela of the entity that governs supernatural creatures here."

The way she put it made the Friends of Cryptids sound more muscular than a group of quasi-scientists who cataloged monsters.

"We demand that you follow our rules here in our lands."

An eerie wail came from the side of the island opposite mine. It was a high-pitched cawing, like from a crow—not the kind of sound I'd expect from a giant, hulking ogre.

The cawing grew insistent and aggressive, as if the munuane was trying to scare Angela off.

"Tell me why you came here," Angela said. "The magic I cast that allows you to understand me will enable me to understand you."

68

More high-pitched cawing came from the woods ahead of me, becoming increasingly aggressive. My hands grew numb from adrenaline and fear, but I pushed through the trees toward the sounds. It sounded like Angela would need me.

"Feeding on humans is forbidden here," Angela shouted. "We humans have laws protecting our waters and fishes. We will punish those who break the laws. You are free to hunt and fish, but you must not harm humans."

A loud splash came from the opposite side of the island. It didn't sound like the ogre jumping in; it was the slap of an object hitting the water.

His paddle board?

"Do not come any closer," Angela commanded. "Stop right there!"

I pushed through the thick underbrush as quickly as I could. Now, the ground sloped downward, and the roots of black mangroves rose from the mud. It sucked at my sandals until I was nearly stuck.

A blinding flash came from Angela's direction along with high-pitched cawing.

Then, the sound of frantic paddling receded into the distance.

When I finally emerged from the mangroves onto the west shore of the island, I saw Angela sitting calmly in her canoe, her paddle resting in her lap.

"I think he got the message," she said.

Behind her, silhouetted by the moon, a tall creature on a paddle board made his way across the channel and toward a park on the far shore of the Intracoastal.

"Was he trying to harm you?" I asked.

"No, he tried to intimidate me into retreating, but it was so he could escape. I had hoped I could get information from him so we could determine if he was the killer, but he was too frightened. I need to find him again and communicate more."

"What did he say to you?"

"He said, 'Go away. Leave me alone.' That was it, other than noises meant to frighten me."

"Did you get a good look at him?"

"Yes. I believe he is a munuane, based on the descriptions in the folklore. I took a photo of him, too."

She paddled closer to the island, and I waded into the water to meet her. She held an expensive digital camera, showing me the screen on the rear. It held the brightly lit image of a giant creature, at least eight feet tall, standing on a paddle board, brandishing a paddle like a weapon. The creature was covered in long reddish-brown fur, flecked with gray, and had a gaping, toothless mouth.

What was shocking was the lack of eyes in its head. Instead, it had large eyes on its knees. They squinted against the bright light.

"Did you use a super-powerful flash when you took this?" I asked.

She laughed. "The light you saw was magic pyrotechnics to scare some respect into him. But it also helped with the picture taking."

Now that the excitement had faded, I felt ashamed.

"You did what I wasn't able to do," I said. "You made contact with the munuane and took his photo."

"Don't feel bad. You're new to this game. Plus, I'm a mage,

70

so I have more defensive magic than you. You'll get the hang of this."

"Why do they even need me when they have you?"

"Because you and Luisa operate the botanica, which is a hub of magic, religion, and folklore. You're more likely than I am to come across supernatural creatures. And there's only one of me. There are too many creatures out there for one person to catalog."

"Too many creatures?"

"Oh, yes. You'd be surprised."

I was. "How could that be so in modern America?"

"There have always been many other beings out there that normal humans simply cannot sense. Yes, in the modern era, many of them have gone extinct or into hiding. But many more show up regularly to take their place as the earth's climate changes and other disruptions occur."

"New ones show up?"

"New species or ones we never knew about. We live on a very crowded planet. Humans are a tiny fraction of the conventional and supernatural species that inhabit it. For instance, think of how many insects there are. And microbes. Most of which you're not even aware of. Supernatural and folkloric creatures can be just as difficult to count as the numbers of insects and microbes."

She smiled with joy at this. I wasn't so sure I was happy about it.

"Go get your kayak, and let's return to the park. We have a lot of work to do," she said as she turned her canoe.

Based on what she said about how many supernatural

creatures there were, it sounded like our work would never be done.

In the coming days, that would become frighteningly apparent.

AFTER WE PULLED our boats out of the water and stowed them atop our vehicles, Angela gave me a quick hug goodnight.

"Thank you for leading me to the munuane," she said. "I never would have found him without you."

"You're just saying that to make me feel useful. What do we do next to deal with him?"

"We wait," she said, her face grim in the moonlight. "If there's another murder like the ones we suspect him of, we'll have to track him down and punish or expel him."

"How will we find him? I'm sure he won't return to Beer Can Island."

"Now that I've encountered him in person, I'll develop spells that can help me find him."

I had a desire brewing inside me I hadn't recognized before I blurted it out.

"Will you train me?" I asked. "I'm mostly self-taught because I don't know any witches. Any real witches, that is, besides me. I would like to become more effective. More powerful."

Angela looked at me for a while without answering.

"I'm not an instructor. I'm a librarian who happens to be a mage."

"You had to further your skills and education to become a mage. Who taught you?"

"She is no longer with us." Angela approached me and reached for my face, pinching my cheek like a grandmother. "Yes, I'll train you. A little here and there, because we're very busy, you and I."

"Yes, we are. And thank you."

"We'll begin Friday night. Meet me at my home. I'll text you the address."

I PULLED up Angela's address on my mapping app and was shocked at what came up. I didn't expect an elderly librarian to live in a high-end waterfront home on a large lake. She couldn't have bought it on her wages. As my mind ran through the possible sources of her wealth, I chided myself for being so materialistic. It was none of my business how she afforded the home.

Of course, my mind couldn't shake the possibility that the Friends of Cryptids had something to do with it.

My visit tonight was about magic, not money, I reminded myself. Still, when I drove through her neighborhood and saw all the brand-new McMansions that had recently replaced older, more modest homes, my nosy mind began churning again.

Until I saw two police cars down the street I was planning to enter. This wasn't a neighborhood where I'd expect to see police activity on a Friday night. That would be Matt's neighborhood.

I slowed down and rolled toward the curve where the road met the lake, and the waterfront homes began. The police cars were parked in front of one of those houses. Their strobe lights weren't on. They were probably there because of a false alarm.

I passed them and looked for Angela's home. But, according to my mapping app, I had already passed it. I pulled into a driveway and turned around, retracing my route.

My stomach clenched. Angela's house was the one with the police cars.

What was the proper etiquette for visiting a home when the police were there? I couldn't just go up and ring the doorbell while the police were conducting their business.

So, I pulled to the side of the road, turned off my lights, and waited.

I waited for what seemed like forever. Now, I was twenty minutes late. Maybe I should text Angela.

But as I started typing, Angela's front door opened, and light flooded her front lawn. From out of the light came two police officers, a man and a woman.

Walking between them on the way to the cars was Angela.

CHAPTER 8

PRESS CONFERENCE, TAKE TWO

Chief Dullart had learned his lesson from the previous wayward-toupee press conference. This time, he held the event in the lobby of Jellyfish Beach's small police headquarters.

"Lobby" was too generous a term. It was more of a waiting room with a front desk, an assortment of flags behind it, and plastic chairs where unfortunate citizens sat waiting for whatever reason they had to be there. Today, the chairs had been arranged in rows facing a podium that had been brought in for the press conference. The chief stood at the podium, flanked by the same two officers as last time, again serving no purpose other than as visual frames for the chief.

Rather than watching on TV, I was here in person, Matt having tipped me off about the presser. Despite several calls to the police station to ask why Angela had been detained, they wouldn't tell me. Of course, I wasn't her lawyer or a family member. I was just a coworker, in a way. Coming here in person was the least I could do as I anguished over Angela's situation.

I was claustrophobic, though. Usually, at a police press conference in Jellyfish Beach, the "press" would only be Matt, or one of the other reporters at the local paper. Occasionally, a reporter from a nearby larger city would show up. TV news crews almost never attended, unless the presser was about a particularly juicy murder, which rarely occurred in this town, until recently. Now that we'd had four deaths attributed to eco-terrorists, we offered a guarantee of good ratings. Consequently, the room was packed with reporters and cameras. I wanted to slip outside for air but was trapped in the corner.

"Thank you all for coming today," Chief Dullart said. His toupee looked secure, and he had only one food stain on his tie. "I'm pleased to announce we are interrogating a person of interest, a member of a group of environmental terrorists, who we suspect has claimed four lives."

Murmuring broke out in the room. I was shocked. How could they accuse Angela of being involved? That was crazy.

"Is it true this person is the local librarian?" a reporter asked.

"Yes, she is," the chief replied. "While secretly being a member of this nefarious organization."

"What organization?"

"We don't know the name, but we've had our eyes on them for quite some time. We believe they were also involved in a fire that caused severe damage at a laundromat in town."

Oh, no. He's referring to an incident when Angela battled a demon and rescued Carl, the friendly zombie.

A horrible possibility struck me: could the group he referred

76

to be the Friends of Cryptids Society? If the police looked too closely at them, they would uncover a host of secrets that would jeopardize the entire supernatural community.

"What evidence do you have tying the librarian to the murder?" asked a different reporter.

The chief laughed. "I can't make that public, Kevin. You ought to know better."

It was a good question, though. It was absolutely insane to believe Angela would have any reason to kill the fishermen and gator hunters. Even though she was a surprisingly lethal force for a little old librarian, thanks to her magic.

I knew nothing about her views concerning the environment. She'd never given me any sign. I just couldn't believe she would have any beliefs extreme enough to lead to violence. Except against monsters that were a danger to the community.

Unless her definition of monster was much broader than mine.

No, I had to stop thinking this way. She couldn't be guilty.

"We're certain of her guilt," the chief said, "but have not charged her yet."

A disturbance came from just outside. The crowd was jostled as someone forced his way into the building. The officers flanking the chief ceased their role as stage props and moved toward the door to stop the intruder.

It would be great drama if the person pushing through the crowd was here to announce the solution to the mystery, but no such luck.

It was a little old man wearing thick glasses and a campaign T-shirt from three presidents ago. He bulldozed his way to the chief's podium.

"What's all the fuss going on here?" he asked in a squeaky voice, looking at the crowd. "I'm here to report a crime."

"You're interrupting my press conference," the chief said. "Report your crime to the sergeant standing over there by the door."

"It's not *my* crime. It's my wife's crime."

"I don't care about her crime. I'm giving a press conference. If you continue to embarrass me in public, you'll be arrested."

"My wife was beating me. That's assault and battery. You guys need to do something about it."

"I need to put you in jail for being in my camera shot. You're disrespecting the chief of police."

"You say you're the police, but doesn't anyone here punish crime?"

"Sir, please come outside," the sergeant said. "I'll take your statement after the press conference."

"You already heard my statement. My wife was beating me."

"No, I wasn't," said an angry female voice. "I was smacking you upside your head."

The old but formidable woman, presumably the man's wife, pushed through the crowd to her husband in front of the podium.

She slapped him on the head with a scuba flipper.

"That's what I was doing. Not beating—smacking. Like this."

She smacked him again.

"Did you see that?" the old man shouted. "She's doing it in front of all these witnesses." He finally noticed the TV cameras. "On Channel Five, too!"

The chief's lieutenants finally intervened and pushed the man away from the podium. But they hadn't yet removed him from the room.

The wife resumed slapping her husband on the head with the flipper, the TV cameras following every smack.

This was getting ridiculous. I quickly cast a sleep spell and the belligerent couple dropped into the arms of the officers, who finally dragged them away.

"As I was saying," the chief said, trying to resume his presser. "Hey, I'm over here."

The TV cameras swung back in his direction.

The chief continued, "We believe we are close to bringing down the nefarious terrorist organization. Expect arrests to occur soon. And thank you for coming today."

He gave his best smile to the cameras, made an about-face, and marched through an interior door, flanked by his lieutenants.

I found Matt nearby and asked him if this was normal for a press conference.

"Normal? Nothing in Jellyfish Beach is ever normal."

As EXPECTED, my doorbell rang soon after I returned home, and I let the two gray-suit-clad partners into the house. Their faces were uncharacteristically distressed.

"Our local enforcer has been detained," said Mr. Lopez.

"I know. I saw it happen. What are you going to do about it?"

"The Society's attorneys will help her," Mrs. Lupis said.

"However, this situation is much graver than our usual legal problems."

"Have members ever been arrested?"

"It's rare, but it happens," Mr. Lopez said. "Some enforcers don't know magic and use conventional weapons. Police departments aren't happy when their citizens launch surface-to-air missiles."

"Our attorneys are good and usually get them released without charges. However, Angela being in custody is quite concerning."

"Quite concerning," Mr. Lopez echoed.

"We believe the police suspect Angela works for the Society."

"In his press conference, the chief said they're investigating a 'terrorist organization,'" I told them.

The two partners exchanged dismayed glances.

"I don't know how this could have happened," Mrs. Lupis said.

"Why would Angela or the Society have come to the police's attention," I asked, "other than the attack by the demon at the laundromat? As I understand it, nothing incriminating was recorded by the security cameras at the location. I believe members of the Knights Simplar were charged for it."

"There was also an incident with a chupacabra last month," Mr. Lopez said.

"Oh, my."

"My words exactly," said Mrs. Lupis.

"The beast was attacking cows at a farm west of town. It stumbled upon some magic mushrooms growing on the cow patties and ate them, going berserk. Angela had to subdue it immediately. Unfortunately, a 'Florida Man' was there—you know the type who's in the news for stealing a police car while drunk, naked, and carrying a baby alligator. He was also partaking of the mushrooms." Mr. Lopez covered his eyes with exasperation. "Florida Man saw the chupacabra and what Angela did to it. We hoped the man would assume what he saw was a psilocybin-induced hallucination, but you never know. Angela helped us deport the creature from Florida, but the damage was done. The police may have heard about the incident."

"How?" I asked. "Florida Man reported it?"

"It was quite a scene with Florida Man and the chupacabra going berserk together. Hideous screams, stampeding cows. There may have been other witnesses."

"Oh, my."

"We must exonerate Angela," Mrs. Lupis said.

"Without getting the munuane blamed," Mr. Lopez added.

"What if there really are eco-terrorists behind this?"

"For us, that would be wonderful," said Mr. Lopez while Mrs. Lupis nodded in agreement. "And you will help us find them."

"Me?"

"I would think you'd gladly accept this mission."

"Um, yeah. But maybe not so gladly."

The partners insisted they had urgent matters to attend to and left. I sat in my kitchen with no clue of how to proceed. So, I called Matt for help.

"You really think the police would mistake the Friends of Cryptids Society for a terrorist group?" he asked.

"No. I think they're using terrorism as an excuse to go after them, even if they don't fully understand what the Society does."

"They wouldn't have arrested your friend with no evidence."

"Maybe they concocted some. They could be more interested in taking down the Society than solving the murders."

"You're giving Chief Dullart too much credit," Matt said. "He's not that bright."

"I know he's not. Hopefully, Angela's attorney will find out how much the police know. In the meantime, we need to find out who killed those men."

"*We?*"

"In the words of Mr. Lopez, 'I would think you'd gladly accept this mission.' It's right up your alley. You know— monsters and evil humans."

"Yeah, that's what I'm all about. It's even on my résumé."

"Don't be sarcastic. You know you love working with me."

"You sure know how to manipulate a guy."

"I'm a witch. Want to see me *truly* manipulate you?"

"No thanks. I'll meet you tomorrow for breakfast at seven. I have some old clippings you should see."

"Hey, Missy," Luisa said over the phone. "I finally found out what happened to my cousin and her husband, Dave."

"The guy from the wedding who I thought lost his soul?"

"Yeah. Well, he's still alive. They moved to Tallahassee. He's a lobbyist now for some chemical company that keeps poisoning poor neighborhoods. He lobbies the state legislature to not regulate the chemical company, so their profits don't get hurt."

"Then he really did lose his soul, and it was replaced by something demonic."

"I think it's more believable that he simply made a career change," Luisa said. "Not everything is a question of good and evil."

She was right. Dave was just an amoral guy. Who was I to judge him? It was time to reconsider Don Mateo's soul-stealing theory of the defilements.

If the black magic was ineffective, did it really matter if my mother was involved?

CHAPTER 9
FRANK'S FRIENDS OF FLORIDA

"Well, that was certainly unpleasant," Angela said when I answered her call.

"Angela! Are you out?"

"I'm home, yes. They kept me at the police station all night and half of today. Can you believe that? In a horrible conference room with outdated furniture and silly motivational posters on the walls."

"Isn't that better than an interrogation room?"

"I don't believe they have one of those. It's not much of a police force we have here in Jellyfish Beach. Makes me wonder if they ever solve any crimes. The questions they asked me were so stupid. Can you believe I was there for three hours before they offered me any water? How rude!"

"Yes. Rude," I said, waiting for her to calm down. "Who interviewed you?"

"The chief and a detective named Marty Glasbag. I've known Marty since he was a school kid, always causing trouble

GET OGRE YOURSELF

in the library. It was reasonable to predict he would end up a criminal. He didn't, but I wish I could say he turned out to be successful. After all, he's the senior detective, but he seems to be as much of a brat now as he was then."

"Tell me what they asked you. Do they believe you killed the fishermen?"

"They asked about my whereabouts when the victims were killed, but the questions were perfunctory. They seemed more interested in whether I'm a member of any radical groups."

"Are you?"

"When would I find the time to do that? The library and the Society keep me too busy."

"Do you think this is about the Society? Is there any way the police could know about it?"

Long pause. "They don't talk about it directly, but I sense they suspect a group is behind some unexplained incidents that have come to their attention."

"Like the fire at the laundromat? Lord Arseton and the Knights Simplar were blamed for that."

"Yes, but Arseton tried to blame you and me. And there was an incident with a chupacabra and magic mushrooms not long ago."

"Yes. Mr. Lopez and Mrs. Lupis told me about it."

"When there are monster encounters, the police are often called. Even if we're perfectly tidy and leave no evidence of monsters, the police can become suspicious."

"What about the Knights Simplar?" I asked. "Do you think they're behind the murders? Do you think the police suspect them?"

"That possibility occurred to me, and I brought it up to the

85

police more than once. They didn't ask me any follow-up questions whenever I mentioned those morons. Which leads me to believe the police don't think they're involved."

"What should we do now? Is the Society in danger?"

"We need to clear up any suspicion of me, of course. And somehow end the killings, so the police will lose interest in the Society. In the meantime, it might be in danger."

THE NEXT DAY, Matt and I met at our usual café facing the beach. Though it was early, there were several people arriving at the beach. I recognized Thong Man from the first press conference. He wore a shirt as he strolled toward the surf, but his thong revealed his very tan buttocks. Isn't there a law against that?

"Ah, the moon is rising over Jellyfish Beach," Matt said. "That guy should worry about skin cancer."

"You have those clippings you were telling me about?" I asked, all business. I sipped my tea in hopes it would jolt my exhausted brain into action.

Matt dropped a pile of paper onto the table—printouts from the newspaper's archives.

"We have lots of environmental groups here in Florida. This state has a remarkably diverse and rare ecosystem, but developers are allowed to run rampant and pave over it. None of the environmental groups is known to be violent. But there have been cases of sabotage at building sites."

"No murders?"

"None attributed to those groups."

I pointed to the stack of paper. "Has my old friend Frank been up to any mischief lately?"

Frank Fitzwhizzle was the leader of Frank's Friends of Florida. The group was known for protesting developers who sought to turn pristine wilderness into subdivisions. The worst crimes they'd committed were petty vandalism and chaining themselves to excavators.

The exception was when Frank got involved with the cockamamie international movement to liberate garden gnomes. Usually, this meant stealing them from people's yards and "setting them free" in the woods. Frank went too far and hired a black-magic sorceress to cast a spell to free the gnomes. It went terribly wrong when the gnomes became animated and attacked the humans who oppressed them.

"Frank's group hasn't been active lately. And he hasn't done anything criminal since he had his run-in with you."

Yes, I summoned a real gnome to teach Frank a lesson. I didn't witness the "lesson," but the gnome told me it was painful for Frank.

"We should pay him a visit. He probably knows the scuttlebutt of any clandestine activities his and the other groups are up to."

"What makes you think he'll speak with us?" Matt asked. "Last time he did, he ended up getting a beat-down from a gnome."

"I'll use my truth-telling spell on him again."

"If he lets you near him."

I often felt guilty using the truth spell on people. It seemed unfair to take advantage of them without their consent. I reserved its use for people I knew were lying or had other bad intentions. Frank had crossed the line when he enlisted black magic for his illegal acts, so he was fair game then and now.

FRANK HAD one of those doorbell cameras, so he saw who we were and didn't have to answer the door. Of course, the promise I made into the camera to donate a thousand bucks to his organization might have warmed his heart to us.

"Welcome, friends," he said as he opened the door. His expression, behind his big white beard, was anything but welcoming.

Frank was probably in his early sixties, but looked much older. It hadn't been that long since I'd last seen him, but time had not been kind to him. I hoped the gnome wasn't to blame.

"Sorry. I was joking about the donation," I said. "We just need to ask you a few questions."

He sighed, and his shoulders slumped in defeat.

"Yeah. What do you want to know?" He remained in the doorway, not inviting us inside.

"Did you hear Jellyfish Beach Police believe eco-terrorists are responsible for recent murders, including an explosion on a charter fishing boat?"

Frank's face blanched.

"No. My group would never, ever commit violence."

"No, not directly," I said sarcastically.

"Not with magic, either. Not anymore." The poor guy's eyes looked haunted.

"Do you know of any groups who could have done this?" Matt asked.

Frank scratched his unruly white hair, which had become sparser since I last saw him.

"There's a new group in South Florida," he said. "What they put on their website seems pretty radical. They never mention violence, but they hint at stopping at nothing to reach their aims."

"What do they call themselves?" Matt asked.

"Nature Under the Spotlight."

"I've never heard of that name," Matt said.

"It's NUTS," I said.

"What is?"

"Their name. The acronym is NUTS."

"They need a better marketing department," Matt said.

"I don't think they have any money," Frank said. "Only their convictions."

Matt furiously finger-tapped his phone.

"Their website is mostly just manifestos. There's hardly any information about the group. No address or phone number, only a link to contact them by email. I'll send one and ask for an interview."

During the conversation, with Frank standing in his doorway, there was no opportunity to cast my truth spell on him. This spell required sprinkling a blend of ingredients upon the subject, which was easy to do beneath a restaurant table, but not out in the open.

While Matt explored the NUTS website on his phone, Frank stepped out onto his front porch to look at Matt's screen. I quickly muttered the incantation under my breath. While Frank was focused on the website, I pretended to look at the phone, too, and moved beside him. Pulling a pinch of the dried herbs, flowers, and various powders from my pocket, I sprinkled it on Frank's shoes unnoticed.

A manic gleam soon appeared in his eyes. He was primed.

"Frank, do you have an issue with fishermen?" I asked.

"I think fishing is barbaric, even catch-and-release fishing. But I hate fishermen less than I hate hunters."

"What about gator trappers?"

"They're evil."

"Would you kill one if you caught him in the act?"

"No. I told you I'm non-violent."

My truth spell forces people to tell the truth; it gives them permission. Most people want to unburden themselves of the truth and recant their prevarications. Even pathological liars, who sometimes convince themselves their lies are true, want relief from the mental contortions they create to live with their lies. I trusted that Frank's answers were true.

"Have you ever killed anyone?"

"Yes."

"One, or more than one?"

"I can't count. There were too many."

"Really?" I did not expect this.

"Yeah. Lots of insects and rodents that had gotten into my house. That was before I became enlightened."

"I meant people. Have you killed any people? Recently, or before you became enlightened."

"All living creatures deserve to live just as much as humans do."

Was he resisting the spell?

"Humans, Frank. Have you killed any humans?"

He began to cry. "Only the people who died because I paid

the sorceress to bewitch the garden gnomes. I didn't mean for that to happen."

"It's okay, Frank," I said, patting his arm. "When you play around with black magic, people get hurt. One last question: do you know who killed these recent victims?"

I rattled off the names of the victims and the circumstances of their deaths.

"No." He wiped away his tears.

"Thank you."

I broke the spell, and Frank immediately stepped away from us and back into the doorway.

"I've got to go now." He closed the door in our faces.

WITH ALL THAT was on my mind, thoughts of Philip and Dorita kept returning to me. I felt so sad and empty after having failed them.

I reminded myself that they had each other for eternity. Dorita hadn't descended too far into dementia. At least, that was the impression they gave. But her "bad days" must be unpleasant if they sought help from me.

As a mortal human, I feared Alzheimer's and other causes of dementia more than almost any other disease. That's what shook me up so much when I thought about the couple.

It was also why I spent more time than I should tinkering with ideas for a better spell.

My recollection spell required no magical ingredients or rituals. It was all organic energy and mental concentration. I guess you could call the invocation a ritual. Who knows how much the words themselves enabled the magic, versus the psychological effect they had on me, helping me create the magic by myself?

I realized the driving force behind the recollection spell was the *desire* to remember, such as the time I blanked out during the written test portion of my nursing-license recertification. And when I used the spell on the woman who witnessed the church defilement, she sincerely wanted to remember, even if it meant reliving the horror of encountering the imp.

Desire—that was the key. I had an idea.

Philip Pound answered the door with a haggard expression.

"Is this a bad day?" I asked.

He nodded. "She's lying down now. She's exhausted from all the verbal abuse she gave me."

"I'm so sorry."

"This doesn't happen too often, but when it does, it kills me inside. I keep telling myself that she won't get any worse, at least, thanks to her becoming a vampire. But her condition has put such a strain on our relationship. I just wish I could have the real Dorita back."

"I'll try my very best," I said. "If you'll put up with my strange requests."

He arched his eyebrows questioningly.

"May I have a lock of your hair?" I asked.

"Of course."

"I'll also need to borrow a photo from your wedding. And

your wedding ring. Don't worry, I'll return them in a couple of days."

As I snipped his hair, I glanced at the wall of the dining alcove. It was covered with small, framed photos, most of which were black and white. They went back far into history.

"You got married after photography was invented, right?"

He laughed. "Just barely."

He pulled a picture from the wall. It appeared to be from the mid-1800s. A young man in formal wear and a young woman in a voluminous wedding dress stared woodenly at the camera.

"You guys were adorable."

He smiled, and a flash of color appeared in his deathly white cheeks.

I scanned the rows of pictures. The only ones in color were of Philip and Dorita posing with other vampires at Squid Tower. The bleached-out images were overexposed due to the use of flashbulbs. I guessed they were shot in the 1960s or '70s.

On the row where the wedding photo had been was another formal photo of the couple, but in this one, Dorita held a baby. Another photo was of the couple with a young boy. The adjacent photo was of a young man posing in a Civil War uniform.

"Did your son survive the war?"

"He did."

"Did he become a vampire?"

"No. He led a normal human life. He lived until 1918 and left behind four children and thirteen grandchildren."

Philip stared at the soldier portrait wistfully.

"May I borrow that photo, too?"

He nodded and handed it to me.

"Thank you, Mr. Pound. I'll get back to you if I have luck creating a new spell."

"Is it really a matter of luck?"

"No. It's a matter of love."

I CONSULTED WITH MY "BRAIN TRUST" at home. Tony reassured me I was on the right track. Don Mateo coached me on how to extract emotions from objects.

Phillip's hair, for instance, contained traces of his energy. It also contained the scent his wife had savored and the texture she had stroked. He was whom Dorita loved most.

The wedding photo contained energy from over a century and a half of being stared at fondly by a loving couple reliving memories. The same was true for the photo of their beloved son.

The desire to remember would be the basis for my spell— the desire to remember the ones you loved and to cherish all the moments you spent with them.

Enhancing Dorita's memory, I hoped, would ease other symptoms of her dementia, if only temporarily. If only on her "bad days."

I extracted the energy from these powerful emotions and wove strands of it together into the complex structure of the spell.

As promised, I used the spell to infuse the magic into a simple solution of water, herbs, and spices.

My description makes it sound easy, but it wasn't. Thanks

to mistakes, I had to tear it apart and reweave it together three times. But when it was ready, I knew it in my bones.

I also knew it in my memory. Yes, I tried it on myself.

Even though it was custom made for Dorita, its power stimulated my brain into remembering a few scenes from early childhood that I had long forgotten. Moments of being loved by parents, occurring long before I knew they had adopted me. And long before my magic gene had begun to influence me.

It was the only normal time of my life.

CHAPTER 10
SHE'S NUTS

"I've got good news and bad news," Matt told me over the phone as I stocked shelves at the botanica. We'd just received a shipment of freeze-dried newt eyes, and I was stocking them in the witchcraft section.

"Tell me the bad news first. I always prefer it that way. Must have come from being a nurse."

"Okay. The president of NUTS—her name is Harriet—doesn't want to meet us."

"And the good news?"

"She loves email and is very loquacious. I'll forward you our email chain."

"I can't get to it just yet. Can you summarize?"

"Somehow, they know about the munuane, although they don't know it by that name."

"That's not good. How do they know about it?"

"Harriet had a run-in with it. You need to read the emails."

As soon as I finished stocking the eyes of newt and several

packages of toes of frog, I sat down in the back room and opened my email on my phone.

Yes, Harriet was a prolific email writer. Brief questions from Matt were followed by multi-paragraph answers filled with science, philosophy, and politics. Harriet was highly intelligent. Too bad she hadn't figured out the unfortunate acronym of her group's name.

Wading through her dense text, I pieced together the story. Harriet had been collecting water samples in the wildlife preserve, not far from where the gator hunters were found. She planned to test the water for its levels of phosphorus and nitrogen, pollutants resulting from agricultural fertilizer runoff. As the daylight was fading, she saw an unusual sight.

A hulking, hairy creature came around the bend of the creek, standing atop a paddle board. Though it was exceptionally tall, the creature could use normal paddles because his arms were so long. She moved her canoe behind a thicket of trees and watched unseen as the creature shot a bow and arrow into the water. The arrow had a string attached, which he used to retrieve it from the water with a large bass impaled upon it. The creature slipped the bass into a sack and paddled farther down the creek. When he passed her, she saw his eyes were located on his knees.

This was apparently too much for her—a hideous monster spearfishing from a modern paddle board. She went on for several pages about how it must be a skunk ape—the Florida version of a Sasquatch—that had suffered congenital mutations caused by manmade pollution.

Later, she concluded the creature was responsible for the murders of the gator hunters she had read about in the news.

When Matt asked her if she knew anything about the other murder and the explosion on the fishing boat, she speculated the creature was responsible for those, too, though her explanation of his motive didn't make sense.

I was not happy that someone else knew about the munuane. If word got out, the creature would be hunted by curiosity seekers and people who wanted to kill it.

Matt and I hadn't investigated environmental groups thoroughly enough to rule them out as the murderers, but it looked as though we were back to square one. The munuane appeared to be the likely killer of the sportsmen, with its fate and that of Angela at serious risk.

We had to capture the munuane.

Captain Rivas looked up at us dubiously as we stood on the dock. Matt and I were waiting when he returned to his boat slip after a morning fishing trip. He knew we were up to weirdness again.

"You still haven't caught the munuane?" he asked.

"No, we haven't," I said. "I've never caught a munuane before, so I don't have the technique down. Munuanes aren't like grouper."

He grinned, not offended by my sarcasm.

"We were wondering if you've heard anything at the marina about him, or if you've sighted anything unusual."

"No. I heard you guys chased him off Beer Can Island. I bet he's somewhere inland, in the swamps, far from people."

While Rivas secured his boat lines to the dock cleats, I

noticed his hull had been patched up with no sign of the bullet holes. It was a professional job; you would never know the holes had been there.

Rivas looked at me, as if to ask why we were still hanging around.

"Excuse me," he said. "I have to hose off my boat and clean my fish so I can deliver them to seafood stores. I can't be late, or someone will beat me to it. With this economy, stupid amateur fishermen try to sell their catch to the seafood markets."

He grumbled and went about his work, ignoring us.

We were at a dead end, and only magic would help us find the munuane. And I knew of only one magician who could do it.

I SOMETIMES REFERRED to myself as a kitchen witch—one who dabbled in herbs and potions, casting her spells literally in the kitchen. There were also hedge witches, green witches, crystal witches, and countless other varieties. What I really was, though, was an elemental witch—deriving my power from my innate magic mixed with energies from the five elements of water, air, earth, fire, and spirit.

Angela was an elemental witch times ten. Years of training had advanced her past my level to the rank of mage. She could harness more powerful energies, like those flowing through ley lines and radiating from the core of the earth. She said she regularly harvested energy from the sun and stars—an ability I was eager to learn someday.

"Why do you want to advance your skills?" she asked me as

we sat in the loft space at the top of the stairs on the second floor of her home—the home I was interrupted from visiting when the police had taken her into custody the other night.

I'd always questioned the utility of lofts when I first shopped for a home. They were too open to serve as a private office and would be too loud if kids were playing up there. Now, I realized lofts made a perfect spot for casting spells, allowing you to draw all the energy in the house easily. I wondered if homebuilders knew that.

"Why do I want to advance my skills? I thought every witch wanted to do that," I replied.

"Not true. Many witches are happy with what they can do. Just like many cooks have their repertoire of recipes and aren't interested in doing the work of advancing their skills."

"As a nurse, I always took classes and additional training to earn higher certifications. It's how I worked my way up to becoming an ICU nurse."

"Power is alluring, but it's not an end in itself. It can be deceptive and dangerous." Angela searched my eyes for the truth.

"With more power, I can heal my patients better. Working at a botanica is not my life's purpose. It's just a better way to earn a living than being a home-health nurse. But I still have patients who need me. Supernaturals can't go to human doctors. I'm all they have. And without being able to use the technology of a hospital, I need magic to heal many of their ailments. The more power I have, the more I can heal."

Angela continued searching my eyes, as if she wasn't certain of my sincerity.

"Humans have always lusted after power. Not always for

the right reasons. As you know, power can corrupt, just as the lust for it can lead you astray."

"I know. My birth mother, whom I'd never met until a couple of years ago, is a black-magic sorceress. She took what she believed was an easier route to more power and ended up corrupted by evil."

"Exactly." Angela nodded. "Yet, even if you stick with white magic, seeking power for the sake of power is not a good thing. Too many magicians manipulating the power of the universe for their own ends upsets the natural order. That can create unimaginable dangers—not just for the magicians, but for everyone on earth."

"I want power so I can do good," I said, beginning to doubt myself slightly. Was I certain my ego wasn't involved? Were my intentions purely altruistic?

I reassured myself that they were.

"Larger communities than ours have councils or guilds to regulate the practice of magic," Angela said. "Even so, there is no global authority limiting the number of magicians in the world. We must regulate ourselves. That's why I'm asking you these questions. I agreed to teach you, but I need to know how much and how far to advance you."

"We can take it one step at a time. Tonight, we need you to do what you can to find the munuane. It's not a magic lesson."

"Simply being with me when I conjure magic will be a lesson in itself." She snapped out of her contemplative mood and stood. "It's time to get to work."

I was eager to see what kind of spell she would use. My locating spells could be effective but were limited.

Angela went to the corner of the loft and unlocked an

ancient wooden armoire. Though her house had a contemporary interior design, the table I sat at and the other furnishings in the loft were all antiques. All, except the lamps, appeared to be centuries old.

The doors of the armoire creaked open. Angela removed a wooden staff made from a tree branch.

"Wow. A wizard's staff?" I asked.

"No, silly. A mage's staff. We use staffs and wands just like wizards do."

This was news to me. I'd only met a couple of wizards and mages before, and they weren't local. Living in tiny Jellyfish Beach kept me isolated from the magic community, except for people I interacted with online or the customers who came to the botanica. All our witch customers were less advanced than I am.

"When I encountered the munuane on the island," Angela said, "I captured a fragment of its energy with this."

She opened a satchel that sat on the table and withdrew the digital camera she'd used that night.

"You took the munuane's photo with this," I said. "You mean the digital image captured its energy?"

Angela laughed. "No. I was briefly close enough to the creature for his energy to be caught on this."

She held up the camera's strap and noticed my puzzled expression.

"It's no ordinary strap. It has silver microfibers woven into it, and I've enchanted it with a spell as sensitive to energy as the camera's sensors are to light. Every time I take a photo of a monster, the strap grabs a bit of its energy, like an adhesive. I'll use the energy in my searching spell."

Angela moved to the top of the stairs and extended her arms to either side, one holding the staff and the other the camera strap. She obviously didn't bother working within a magic circle on the floor like I did. I guess she was too big-league for that.

Angela hummed a tune, low notes coming from deep in her throat. The melody was strange and ancient, but somehow familiar. It made goosebumps break out on my arms.

Soon, the air became charged with static electricity, and the hairs on the back of my neck rose. As a witch myself, I was sensitive to the flow of energy from the earth, and I sensed it pouring into Angela.

Her staff and the camera strap glowed with purple light. The floor vibrated beneath my feet. I had to look twice to confirm that Angela now hovered two inches above the floor.

"Come here," she said. "Touch me."

I approached and placed a hand on her back. It was like touching a live wire.

My vision went dark, and I was briefly afraid, until gradually an image filled my head—an ocean beach, viewed from above, as if from a bird's eyes. This must be what Angela was seeing now.

I recognized the section of beach, just north of Jellyfish Beach, where there were no condo towers, only very expensive homes. It was where I had found the ogre footprint.

The flapping of wings at the edges of the vision confirmed that we were seeing through the eyes of a seagull. It glided lower until it hovered above a monstrosity of a house that some billionaire had built to resemble a Renaissance-era European palace. The bird hovered outside the massive two-story-tall windows that faced the ocean.

Then the vision faded, and I was staring at Angela's back. She lowered her arms, and everything was normal again.

"Do you recognize the house?" she asked.

"Yes." I explained finding the footprint nearby. "But what I don't understand is what on earth an ogre from the South American jungle is doing inside an oceanfront mansion?"

"Doing what anyone would do. Enjoying the ocean view."

CHAPTER II
OCEANFRONT OGRE

The front of the mansion faced Highway A1A, the road that paralleled the beach along the entire Atlantic coastline of Florida. As befitted a gaudy mansion, it was blocked off by an enormous stone wall and fancy wrought-iron gate. Which was locked. I know because I checked. I hoped the munuane wasn't staring out the window at the time and didn't know how to check security-camera footage.

I parked the car at a public beach about half a mile away, and Angela and I walked down the beach to the mansion's rear. The two-story windows were covered with curtains. Hopefully, that meant the owners were out of town, which would explain why the munuane was hiding there.

We climbed a dune, staying out of sight behind low sea-grape trees, and beheld a massive, tiled patio area and swimming pool. It was bordered by a narrow lawn that ended in the dunes. At the edge of the lawn was a low fence, not even tall enough to keep anyone out. Presumably, the homeowners didn't want an ugly fence marring their view of the breakers.

"I'm assuming there are security cameras everywhere," I said. "Probably motion detectors, too."

"They must be off," Angela said. "Otherwise, how would the munuane get inside without setting off an alarm that called the police?"

"If the alarm is on, can you disarm it with your magic?"

"Probably. I have a spell or two that can disable it. If not, I can blast it with enough energy to fry the system. Let me check to see if it's on."

Angela had brought her staff along, her version of heavy weaponry. She closed her eyes and extended her arms toward the mansion, holding the staff horizontally in both hands. Blue light appeared at both ends of it, then faded away.

"The alarm is not on," she said.

"Should we sneak up like ninjas?"

"He will know that we're here whether we sneak or not. Let's go."

We walked along a short trail through the dunes and reached the gate of the four-foot-tall white metal fence. The gate was unlocked.

We reached the patio and walked around the amoeba-shaped swimming pool, with a whirlpool on one end and a waterfall on the other. The water was flowing, but everything else on the patio was out of commission. The wooden lounge chairs were stacked off to the side, and the cushions were put away somewhere. Yes, the owners were out of town.

Angela marched right up to a French door and tried the handle. It was locked, of course.

"I'll take this one," I said. "It's the least I can do."

Though my spells to open locks were among my least competent, I put all my efforts into it, hoping to impress Angela. The bolt clicked open a minute later.

We walked into a cavernous space, with sheer white drapes covering the tall windows. This appeared to be the casual family room, but it was larger than my entire house, with modern furniture grouped in several seating areas and a television larger than a stadium scoreboard.

Angela froze and so did I. A scuffling sound had come from the room next door. She grasped her staff defensively, and I could feel the power surging through it.

She walked through the room toward the sound. I followed her, my heart hammering, while I conjured a protection spell to surround the two of us. I suspected, though, that Angela wouldn't need it.

We walked silently through the family room. Angela paused at a doorway with its pocket doors open. Then she passed through, with me right behind.

This room was a dining room—also two stories tall. An intricate crystal chandelier hung above a light-brown Scandinavian wooden table that was large enough for twelve. No one was here.

The creature was in the house, though. So, we kept going, passing through a butler's pantry large enough for a passel of butlers, and into a kitchen that was gigantic and filled with two of every appliance and feature you could imagine.

My eye barely caught movement behind one of the islands. Something tall, brown, and shaggy had slipped through a door on the opposite end.

"Did you see that?" I whispered.

Angela nodded. She picked up her pace to catch up with the creature.

Leaving the room, we passed another pantry and went down a hallway lined with closed doors. Angela swung her staff back and forth like a dowsing rod, using it to detect the munuane's energy.

The hall ended in the main foyer. It was three stories tall. Why not? A chandelier larger than the one in the dining room hung on a heavy chain descending from the ceiling far above. Two identical staircases rose on either side of the space to a second-story landing. Opposite us was an arched doorway leading into a formal living room. A wide hallway ran between the staircases toward the rear of the home.

Angela's head jerked toward the second-floor landing, and she raced up the stairs, more like a gazelle than a granny. I lumbered up the stairs behind her as best I could.

On the landing, a hallway lined with doors led to a bright window facing the sea. It was bisected by halls extending to the right and left. Immediately in front of us was a staircase rising to the third floor.

How many bedrooms does this place have? And how many housekeepers?

Angela sprinted up the stairs. Panting for breath, I considered taking the elevator beside the stairs, but that would be poor form.

The top floor, smaller than the lower floors, appeared to be dedicated to the master suite. Master complex, to be more accurate. There were many sitting rooms, two baths, and two ludicrously large walk-in closets. The entire space at the rear of the floor was the bedroom. We rushed down the short hall, through the open door, and halted in our tracks.

We'd found the munuane.

But there wasn't only one. There were six of them.

THE MUNUANE we had followed was standing by the bed, while the others got up from chairs around the room's periphery. They were of various sizes, ranging from enormous to gigantic. Each was covered in long, thick brown hair, matted in some places, like long-haired water-dog breeds. They had wide mouths, and hair covered whatever shape their noses were. Their most unnerving characteristic, besides their size, was the location of their eyes on their knees. The shiny black orbs blinked at us.

There was an awkward moment while we and the monsters stared at each other, unsure of what to do. I sensed anxiety among them, but also hostility. They communicated with each other with low grunts, high-pitched squeaks, and the cawing I had heard on the island.

I cast a spell that enabled me to get a basic understanding of foreign languages—not intellectually, but on an emotional level. If a woman spoke to me in Turkish, I couldn't comprehend that she was saying, "Good morning. Isn't the weather lovely today?" However, I would know she was giving me a friendly greeting interspersed with small talk.

Once the spell kicked in, the munuanes' communications came through as a debate whether we were harmless or a danger, and wondering what the heck we were doing in their house. Also, Angela seemed to scare them. I got the vibe that the group was a family: two parents and their young-adult offspring.

"Hello," I said, smiling, even though I didn't know if smiles were friendly for South American ogres. "It's us again!"

I picked up communication between them that was wondering what the human had said. And there was some discussion about eating. I couldn't tell if they were asking what's for dinner, or if they were talking about eating us. Probably the latter.

"Which of them is the one you saw on the island?" I whispered to Angela.

She still stood frozen, holding her staff in a fighting stance. If you think librarians are scary, you wouldn't want to see her like this.

"The big one with gray in his hair."

No surprise. He was definitely male, and the reason I can say that with such confidence does not need to be mentioned. Clearly the father of the family, he also appeared the most dangerous.

"Please don't kill any more humans," I said, rather hopelessly. "It could lead to harm to your family."

"I've been trying to send that message to them with a telepathic spell," Angela said. "No one appears to agree with me. But, honestly, I don't believe anymore that a munuane committed the murders."

The munuane family continued their discussion, then seemed to reach a resolution.

The father's eyes, on his knees, began glowing yellow

around their dark pupils. I remembered seeing those eyes the night Matt and I were at the fishing pier beneath the bridge.

"We need to get out of here," I said, too late.

The father lunged toward us and was met by a bolt of purple lightning from the end of Angela's staff.

"Run!" she shouted to me. "I'll try to hold them off."

"I can't leave you. My protection spell over you will break."

"I've got my own protection spell. Please, go. I'll be right behind you."

The rest of the family moved toward us, and I bolted like a rabbit away from them. The crack of electricity came from behind me, followed by the angry roar of an ogre in pain.

I fell, more than ran, down the stairs all the way to the foyer. There, I paused. I couldn't leave the house without Angela.

The wait was agonizing while the distant sounds of struggle came from the third floor. When it was suddenly silent, with no sign of Angela, I panicked.

Should I go back upstairs? If Angela was incapacitated, I would be helpless before the munuanes. I should have tried my sleep spell or my immobility spell against them before I ran away, though there was a chance they wouldn't work on non-humans. I nervously headed back to the staircase.

A ding from an elevator came from a hallway under the stairs. Angela had won the battle and took the elevator down like a conquering hero?

The four young-adult children poured out of the hallway and raced toward me.

Backing toward the front door, I tried the immobility spell. I was shaking so badly with fear that I almost dropped the power charm I kept in my pocket.

They were upon me before I could finish the spell, punching me in my head and body, slashing me with their claws. My protection spell shouldn't have allowed them to touch me. It obviously had faltered, but there was enough left to curtail their efforts and allow me to wriggle away and stumble out the door and down the front steps.

I raced along the brick driveway toward AIA, in full view of the passing traffic. The munuanes did not come outside after me.

I was bruised, battered, and bleeding. My magic had failed me. And I had failed Angela. She was still inside the mansion, and I didn't know if she was still alive.

What could I do? I had to rescue her, but how?

The front gate was locked, preventing me from leaving the property. The munuanes could have come after me and torn me to pieces, but they must not have wanted to be seen by passing cars. That showed intelligence.

I circled the mansion, looking for ways to sneak back in. I cast my protection spell again, but its earlier failure ruined my confidence that this version would work. Getting Angela out might be a suicide mission, but I had to try. I couldn't leave her in there.

On the beach-facing side of the mansion, I approached the pool area and the French doors we had entered before. I crouched behind a dune and began to build an immobility spell to use against the munuanes. It might not work, but if it slowed them down at all, I could get inside. What happened next would be anybody's guess.

Mere seconds later, before I could build the spell, the door popped open. Two of the younger munuanes emerged and ran toward me. Then, the other two rushed from a door on the side. They swarmed over the dunes, coming at me from my right and left.

I escaped by running toward the surf before turning to my right, to the south, and sprinting where the sand was firmest. The only nearby haven was Squid Tower, about two and a half miles away.

The munuanes didn't follow me for long. They stopped and turned around, returning to the mansion. They must have wanted to avoid being spotted by humans while there was still a bit of daylight remaining. I grudgingly accepted the reality that I couldn't rescue Angela on my own. So, I texted Agnes about what had happened and begged for help. Supernatural assistance was what I needed. I just hoped it wouldn't come too late.

As the sun went down, I reached Squid Tower. Vampires and werewolves were my only hope.

I remembered Angela's last words to me—that she didn't think the munuanes were the murderers. Even if that were true, their innocence wouldn't matter to me one bit if they killed her.

CHAPTER 12

I RECOGNIZED HIS BUTT

When I entered the lobby of Squid Tower, I crossed paths with Walt Whitman.

"Oh, Missy! What a pleasant surprise. I didn't expect you until our creative-writing workshop tomorrow night. I have a new poem I'd like to test out on you. First new one in a hundred and ten years!"

"Sorry, Walt. I'm here on an urgent matter. You can read me your poem tomorrow, assuming I don't have to cancel."

I hurried past him down the hallway that led to the meeting rooms. He followed, curious.

Agnes, former detective Affird, and Harry Roarke waited at a table in the card room. Henrietta, Agnes's assistant, parked her mobility scooter next to Agnes.

"Ah, Missy," Agnes said with a smile. "At last, we can offer you help instead of the other way around."

"I can't tell you how grateful I am. Since going to the police is not an option, you're my only hope. Let me start off by saying

I don't have a plan, just a dire need for help rescuing a friend from a family of ogres."

"We're here to make a plan," said Affird, wearing his shades inside, just like he did when he was alive.

I raced through a narrative about what had happened this afternoon with the munuanes and the murders they were accused of. I could refer to the Friends of Cryptids Society only obliquely, because of my vow of secrecy, but Agnes already knew enough about my obligations to them.

"Do you believe they will harm your friend?" Affird asked in his flat, no-nonsense voice.

"According to the legends, munuanes will eat humans. We need to rescue her right away."

"Where exactly is this mansion?" Harry asked.

I gave him the address. Everyone in the room, except for Walt, recognized the place from my description. Along the stretch of gaudy mansions, this was the gaudiest.

"Who owns the place?" Affird asked as we headed for Squid Tower's parking garage.

"I looked it up on the tax assessor's website before we went there. A Felix Dingledorf. I couldn't find anything about him on the internet."

"Because it's an alias," Affird said. "He's a drug smuggler. Moved up here from Miami-Dade County."

"Probably because law enforcement up here is a bunch of yokels," Agnes said.

Affird glared at her from behind his shades.

"I don't know if Dingledorf knows the munuanes are there, or if they simply broke in because he was out of town," I said,

"But we have to get there as soon as possible—before they harm Angela or change their location."

"What do the legends say about how to kill these ogres?" Affird asked.

"I'd prefer if we didn't kill them," I replied. "But if we must, their eyes are their greatest vulnerability. And their eyes are on their knees."

"Eyes on their knees? That sounds like a ridiculous old wives' tale," Harry said.

"Yeah, as ridiculous as a human turning into a wolf," Affird muttered.

That shut Harry up.

"It's true," I said. "I've seen their eyes."

We reached an old minivan parked on the ground level of the garage. Schwartz was waiting in the driver's seat, and we all piled in.

Affird looked at me. "Can your magic unlock the mansion's doors?"

I nodded.

"I always believed vampires could turn into mist and slip through the cracks of doors," he said. "What a freaking disappointment the truth is!"

"Old wives' tale," Harry muttered.

"You werewolves should go in first and sniff out the creatures' locations. Vampires will guard all the points of egress. If you need backup, we'll come in."

"With your scary fangs?" Harry's sarcasm was too much.

"With our superhuman strength. And these." Affird lifted the bottom of his polo shirt to reveal a pistol in a holster. "To take out their eyes."

THEY WERE old in body age, retired, and supernatural. These strange freaks were my commando team because they were all I had.

Harry led a group of five werewolves who met him at the mansion. They had all shifted to wolf form, so I didn't recognize them, except for Harry with his distinct white coat. The others had various shades of gray and brown, streaked with the white fur of old age.

Affird led a smaller group comprising Schwartz, Sol, and Oleg, a retired cavalry officer from the army of Catherine the Great. The latter two owned more firearms than the average American, which meant more than some armies.

Although Agnes was the nest mother, she put herself under Affird's tactical command. Her only weapons were a long dagger and a spear. Born into Visigoth nobility over 1,500 years ago, she was deadly with a spear.

The team followed me around the mansion's exterior as I unlocked each door with my spell. I was getting better at it with practice, by the way. A werewolf entered each door, waiting on the threshold, while a vampire took up position just outside.

We realized we were one vampire short, until Walt sauntered up and stood outside the last door, a yellowed volume of Longfellow's poems in hand.

"Do you have a weapon?" I asked him.

"The weapon of truth, and the power of beauty."

"Okay, I'd better guard this door with you." I began constructing the framework of my immobility spell so I could finish conjuring it in seconds, if needed. If it worked against ogres, that is.

Now that everyone was in position, we waited for the pre-arranged signal. It was close to midnight, and the clouds shifted westward, revealing a crescent moon. I was the only creature here who wished there was more moonlight for seeing. The crash of the breakers was angry. I tensed with anxiety about what was to come.

The honking cry of a great blue heron was louder than the surf. Only it didn't come from a bird; it was Agnes's signal to attack.

The werewolves disappeared into the darkness of the giant home. My palms sweated as I waited for what would happen.

A short bark came from upstairs. Seconds later, a cacophony of snarls and growls filled the house, followed by thuds of bodies and the crash of a large piece of furniture falling over.

Then came yelps of wolves in pain.

Footsteps pounded toward the door where Walt and I stood sentinel. The footsteps of bipeds.

Walt and I exchanged glances, and he quickly closed the door.

It burst open, knocking him off balance. Two munuanes ran out. The young males. They fled toward the beach while I frantically completed my immobility spell. I cast it toward them as they climbed the dunes.

And you know what? The spell actually worked. At least on one of the munuanes. He froze, completely immobile, at the top of the dune, while his sibling disappeared over the crest and onto the beach.

I ran over to the enchanted munuane. He was smaller than his father, the creature we had originally encountered. This one's fur was sleek with youth, but he appeared to be an adult. His stance was that of an athlete running up bleachers for exercise. He was like a statue; the only movement came from his long fur waving in the ocean breeze.

And from the eyes on his knees, darting back and forth with panic. Taking pity on him, I cast my sleep spell, and soon his eyes closed in repose.

I left him there and hurried back to the mansion. Two wounded werewolves lay on the patio beside the pool, blood trickling onto the tile. One had an arrow penetrating a haunch. The other wolf bled from deep lacerations caused by ogre claws.

Walt knelt beside them, trying but unable to help, his instincts from nursing during the Civil War taking over. So did mine. Though my medical expertise was significantly more advanced than his.

However, the patients didn't need our help. Their werewolf injury-healing powers went to work. The first wolf's flesh expelled the arrow, and the wound closed before our eyes. The other wolf healed just as quickly.

Harry joined us on the patio.

"The mansion is clear," he said. "No sight or scent of anything alive in there."

Once they were fully healed, he and his werewolves bounded off down the beach toward Seaweed Manor, where they could shift back to human form without showing us their naked senior bodies.

Meanwhile, the vampires were still exploring the mansion. After the trauma of my last visit here, I didn't want to go inside.

Finally, Agnes exited the mansion.

"Nice place," she said. "When my husband served King Euric of the Visigoths, the palace was like a dump compared to this."

"Did you find anything?" I asked impatiently.

"There was no sign of your friend. It looks as though the ogres moved out. I'm not sure why the two males stayed behind. Perhaps for reconnaissance. The question is, did they originally gain access by breaking in, or were they invited?"

"Or maybe it's an Airbnb for monsters."

Agnes frowned. "I do not know what that is."

"Never mind. Can we keep the one I captured at Squid Tower until the Friends of Cryptids pick him up? It's impractical for me to bring him to my house."

Agnes hesitated. "Okay. But how long will he remain immobile?"

"I'll need to refresh the spells every six hours or so. It's going to be inconvenient."

Agnes nodded with a knowing look. Yes, she was probably thinking it was very inconvenient for her community to be saddled with my ogre problem.

We all had our burdens to carry in life. Mine happened to be monsters. Few humans could say that.

Once all the vampires had cleared from the mansion, I locked it back up, pocketing a clump of shed munuane fur. My witchy instincts told me it might come in handy.

Then, we had to transport the munuane to Squid Tower before sunrise. We hadn't wanted to park the vampires' minivan right in front of the mansion where it could be seen from A1A. And the public beach parking lot was closed, so the vampires had left the minivan on the road's shoulder, not far away. But first we had to transport the ogre to it.

Vampires have impressive strength, even these who were old in body age. Still, Sol and Oleg whined about having to carry our prisoner who, though he was smaller than his father, was probably a good four hundred pounds.

Instead, I used magic, combined with my innate telekinesis abilities, to levitate the ogre a foot above the sand. We simply pushed him along, as if he were on a dolly.

"Dang, blast it!" Schwartz exclaimed when we reached the minivan. "I got a parking ticket."

"That's the least of our worries," Agnes said.

"I don't see any no-parking signs," Schwartz said. "I'm going to fight this ticket."

"Really? You're going to show up at court in the daytime?"

"I'll hire a lawyer to do it."

"Leo, you're a hundred and seventy-five years old," Sol said. "Your investments have made you rich. Just pay the freaking ticket."

"I'm fighting for the principal of it."

"Shut up, you guys, and help us get this ogre in the minivan," Affird ordered. "Fold the seats down."

"I should've bought a pickup truck. Who knew that one night I would have to transport a gigantic ogre?" Schwartz muttered.

"Where will I sit?" Oleg asked.

"There's no room," Agnes said. "You, Walt, and Sol will have to walk back."

They grumbled for a bit, then set off down the sidewalk at vampire speed. They would arrive at Squid Tower before we did.

The minivan sagged as I broke the levitation spell, and the munuane's full weight settled down. Schwartz got behind the wheel, and Agnes crawled into the passenger seat, while I sat in the back with our prisoner.

"What's that smell?" Schwartz asked.

"A hairy ogre who spends a lot of time in the water. You'll get used to it," I said.

"Never." Schwartz made a U-turn, and we headed back to Squid Tower.

I CALLED the number on Mrs. Lupis's business card. She and Mr. Lopez arrived at Squid Tower just as the orange and purple tones of dawn were filling the sky above the ocean.

Their timing was convenient for them because they had an aversion to vampires. The community was deserted when their large box truck pulled up. Two workers brought out a cage on wheels—the kind a zoo would use to transport a lion—and transported the munuane from the storage room near the swimming pool to the truck.

"How long before your spells wear off?" Mr. Lopez asked me.

"I refreshed them an hour ago. They'll last until early after-noon. You'll be gentle with him, right? You won't use powerful tranquilizers on him, will you?"

"Don't worry," Mrs. Lupis said. "It's not often we have a

monster in custody, but we know how to do it. If we could manage a dragon, we can take good care of this guy."

"We appreciate the opportunity to study a yet-to-be-cataloged monster in depth," Mr. Lopez added.

"You had a dragon?" I asked.

"Yes. A female named Yulia. She stayed with us only briefly —an entirely consensual arrangement to assist us in habitat restoration for her species."

"We understand you have had interactions with dragons," Mrs. Lupis said.

"Yes. A long time ago. I hope their species is doing okay."

Mr. Lopez shrugged. "It's a struggle for any species on this planet nowadays, especially for monsters. Dragons have an alternate world where they take refuge, but we don't have any information about it. Yulia certainly didn't say."

Dragons escaped to the In Between, a place I had visited more than I cared to. A place I will not tell anyone about who doesn't need to know.

"Thank you again for capturing the munuane," Mrs. Lupis said. "We'll notify you when we release him."

After my Society handlers left, I walked to the end of Squid Tower's dune crossover. With the vampires asleep for the day, it was nice and quiet here—a perfect time to relax. I followed the landscaped path to the wooden boardwalk that led to the beach. At its end were two benches facing each other. I sat in one and stared at the ocean. The surf was gentle today, and the beach was empty of passersby at this hour. Taking in a deep breath of salt air, I leaned back and relaxed.

Until I saw the body on the beach.

It was at the base of the dunes, about twenty feet away. At

first, I thought it was headless, but then I realized the head was in a hole in the sand. I hurried down the stairs to the beach and went over to investigate, to see if it was someone I could save, while I fumbled for my phone to call 911.

The man lay face down with his head buried in a sea turtle's nest that had been disturbed. Eggs were scattered beside his head. I reached for his neck and felt no pulse. He had apparently been asphyxiated.

I thought I recognized his butt. No, I'm not joking. These flabby buttocks, revealed by a thong bathing suit he had no business wearing, resembled the ones that had distracted viewers during the police chief's press conference on the beach. I would have to see his face to confirm it was him, but I would be disturbing a crime scene if I pulled his head from the turtle nest.

My trembling fingers finally punched the correct three numerals, and I spent the next several minutes explaining to the operator what I had found.

"You say you think you know him because of his buttocks?" she asked me.

"Never mind. That's not important. Please send someone here before beachgoers show up."

CHAPTER 13
UNDER SCRUTINY

S quid Tower suffered the indignity of having emergency vehicles pour through its gates. Not that any vampires were around to see it. This had happened a few years ago, when murder victims were found on the beach nearby. Having been drained of all their blood, they had appeared to be the prey of a vampire, or vampires, whereas Mr. Thong's demise had the signature of a South American ogre—or of a human who appeared to have the same motive as the munuane: punishing those who abuse the aquatic ecosystem.

Mr. Thong, it appeared, was stealing sea turtle eggs. That was a serious crime, resulting in large fines and jail time. But it shouldn't have brought a death sentence.

Matt showed up shortly after the crime-scene techs began examining the body. He managed to get closer to the scene than the police officers allowed me to get. They'd moved me away from the body when they arrived.

As I had expected, curious beachgoers were gathering,

mostly elderly folks doing their morning walks, but a younger couple wandered over, too. Based on their sickly pale skin, I assumed they were tourists, because vampires wouldn't be out at this hour. The crime-scene techs hung a tarp from light stands to block the civilians' view of the body.

Detective Shortle appeared on the dune crossover where I had been sitting earlier. Shortle was in her late twenties, having been promoted to detective only a year or so ago. She displayed the overconfidence of youth and had given me a lot of attitude in an earlier case when our paths first crossed. Our relationship had improved when I advised her about the church defilements.

After she came down the steps and spoke to the officers at the crime scene, she looked in my direction. She was not smiling.

I gave her a forced smile as she made her way across the sand to me.

"Ms. Mindle," she said, offering her firm hand and shaking mine. "How have you been?"

"Just fine, aside from the trauma of finding him." I pointed to the victim, who was getting zipped up in a body bag. "And you?"

"Busy. After Chief Dullart forced out the interim chief, I've been deep in the weeds. Now, could you give me your account of finding Mr. Massey?"

"How did you get his name? Not much room in his thong to carry a wallet."

"Oh, he's been arrested before."

"For stealing turtle eggs?"

She shook her head no. "Embezzlement. Please go on."

I explained how I found Mr. Massey, making one distortion of fact when I claimed I was at Squid Tower so early because of a home-health visit. I also, of course, left out the mention of my home-invasion crime mere hours ago.

"It's odd that you keep turning up at crime scenes." Shortle wore a white polo shirt with the police-department logo and navy trousers with a holster on her belt. Most detectives in Florida don't wear suits like in the cop TV shows, at least not in Jellyfish Beach. Shortle was pretty, with a strong jaw and nose. She was tall, with narrow hips and muscular arms. She wore her straight black hair long, like I wore my chestnut hair. I wouldn't think a cop would have long hair.

"Pure coincidence," I replied. "Trouble always finds me wherever I am."

"Is there anyone who can vouch for where you were earlier this morning?"

"Yes. They're asleep at the moment, though."

"Did you see anyone on the beach when you found the victim?"

"No. The beach was deserted. I was sitting on a bench up there, enjoying the view. When there was more light, I looked to the north and saw him. I went over to investigate, but it was clear that he was deceased. Was he asphyxiated?"

Shortle looked up from her notepad. She didn't have to answer me, but she nodded. "The medical examiner will determine the cause of death, but it looks like his head was held in the sand, and he couldn't breathe. As if to make a statement about his breeching the turtle nest. Like an eco-terrorist would do."

"One thing's been bugging me. If he was stealing turtle

eggs, why isn't there a bag or something to carry them in? Remember, no pockets in a thong."

She returned to writing notes. "He probably had plastic grocery bags that blew away in the wind."

Of course, it was dead calm this morning with barely a breeze.

"Do you have any ties to environmental groups, Ms. Mindle?"

"I make small donations to some non-profits, but I don't belong to any clubs."

"I see. What about groups that are into, um, spiritual stuff?"

I didn't like where this was going.

"You know I have expertise in spiritual and supernatural stuff. But I'm not involved in any groups related to it. Are you going to ask me if I go to church?"

She reddened. "I'm not interested in your religious beliefs."

"It makes sense that you're asking me about environmental groups. After all, the chief said activists are the prime suspects. But are you saying you don't think they're environmentalists?"

She flipped the cover closed on her notebook and stuffed it in her back pocket.

"I'm not saying that at all."

"I hope you've been keeping an eye on the Knights Simplar," I said. "Has Tim Tissy been indicted for abducting my friend and the other gentleman?"

She nodded. "He's out on bail."

"If you're interested in groups that promote violence," I said, "you should add the Knights Simplar to your list of suspects. They're a bunch of conspiracy theorists who have harassed me and the customers of our botanica. They think we're Satanists, or something. But they're the ones who are into demon worship."

Shortle frowned. "You've already complained about them before."

Well, it seemed like the best way to divert attention away from The Friends of Cryptids Society.

"They could be responsible for the vandalism at the houses of worship," I said, even though I believed my mother was the culprit. "Mostly, they're a group of adults who like to dress up and role play. They would be a harmless joke, except for the fact that they attack people. Surely, they've had complaints filed against them. They even attack furries."

"Furries?"

I had to explain the people who dress up in animal costumes and the entire phenomenon of cosplay with its various forms and the annual conventions. By the time I was done, I had thoroughly baffled Shortle with trivia about the many ways humans use fantasy to seek meaning in life beyond their mundane daily existences. The kookier all these groups and clubs seemed, the less likely it was she would investigate the Friends of Cryptids.

Our attention was diverted as the body bag was carried up the stairs to a gurney waiting on the dune crossover. The crime-scene techs were packing up, and Shortle had a lot of work ahead of her. She thanked me and rejoined the officers.

Matt came over. No hugs or kisses on the cheek from him when he was working.

"You think the munuanes did it?" he asked.

"They were living nearby, so it's possible. The last thing

Angela said before she was captured was she didn't think they're the killers."

"Based on what reasoning?"

"She didn't say. She was too busy being abducted."

"What do you think?"

"It's possible. But we need to find out quickly before more people die and the wrong person is arrested. Detective Shortle has been asking too many questions. I'm afraid she has an inkling about the Friends of Cryptids Society."

When I said that, I didn't know an arrest would come so quickly.

MATT CALLED me the next day before the news went public. Frank Fitzwhizzle, of Frank's Friends of Florida, had been arrested at his home. I did not see this coming, especially since they had previously interviewed Angela.

Matt didn't know what led the police to suspect Frank, aside from his environmental activism, but we would find out at a police press conference this evening.

"The chief sure does like press conferences," Matt said. "He probably wants to become a politician."

"He needs to choreograph his events a little better, so he doesn't look like a fool."

"What do you want? This is Jellyfish Beach."

"But our police can still arrest innocent people and ruin their lives. You saw Frank—he's a mere shell of what he used to be. The most I'd expect him to do is chain himself to a bulldozer like in his glory days. But murder people? No way. He was never violent."

"And the garden gnomes?"

"He did not mean for that to happen. We've been through this already."

Matt sighed. "Promise me you'll keep an open mind. Hold your judgment until you hear what evidence the police have against him."

AFTER SEVERAL SCOLDINGS, Tony agreed not to smoke in the garage anymore. But he also promised to smoke only in the backyard, out of view of my neighbors. We couldn't let anyone know how precocious my iguana was—that he spoke as well as smoked. And with my luck, I'd probably be accused of cruelty to animals, as if I taught him to smoke as part of some roadside carnival stunt.

He paced back and forth across my patio as he puffed, as if wrestling with a mighty philosophical issue.

When he was done, he appeared at my back door like a dog, and I let him into the kitchen.

"I tell ya," he said, "the supernatural atmosphere around here is positively polluted by black magic."

He coughed and cleared his throat.

"You need to quit smoking," I said.

"Stop trying to change the subject. You don't want to hear about the black magic because your mother is involved in it. And you don't want to deal with her."

"You've been reading my mind again."

"I'm a familiar. That's what I do. And again, you're changing the subject. What are you doing to stop the church defilements?"

"I spread the word about Don Mateo's soul-stealing theory to the police. I even broke up a black-magic altar at a church. But I'm doubting that Don Mateo was right."

The wine glasses in my kitchen cabinet fell off their shelves as the door opened and something heavy landed on the counter with a loud thud among the shattered glass.

Don Mateo materialized, blinking in confusion.

"I thought I would arrive in your lingerie drawer," he said. "What is wrong with me?"

"You're not a poltergeist, Don Mateo. Why are you breaking things?"

"Sorry, madam. Something threw me off. Most likely it was all the black magic here in the material plane."

"See?" Tony gloated. "I was right."

"I overheard something about my being wrong," Don Mateo said.

I explained to him about the hedge-fund manager.

"Not only did he survive, but he made a major career change. At first, I thought his line of work showed that his soul had been replaced by an evil one, but he was always that way. I think he kept his original soul."

"Madam," Don Mateo said, slipping off the counter onto the floor without disturbing the broken glass. "You're looking at it the wrong way. Remember, I knew the heretics who employed this black-magic technique in the late sixteenth century. They were not interested in stealing souls to possess the victims' soulless bodies as a demon would."

"Then what happens to the victims who lose their souls?"

"As I told you before, their souls are replaced by others. When your body expires, your soul leaves it, of course. But if your body was alive and healthy without a soul, there are countless disembodied souls that would rush to inhabit your body."

"Ghosts like you?" Tony asked.

"Usually, disturbed souls. Dark souls that crave the opportunity to live human life again."

"So, the guy I was talking about had far from an angelic soul," I said. "When he lost it, a slightly worse soul took its place?"

"Precisely."

"But why? What's the point of taking souls if you're not going to replace them with demonic souls and create an army of evil soldiers?"

Don Mateo laughed. "The heretics simply wanted to collect souls to amass power for themselves. A catastrophic amount of power when in evil hands. That is what I expect the black-magic sorceress is doing today."

"You said 'sorceress.'"

"I did."

"Just accept what you've suspected all along. The sorceress is your mother," said Tony.

He was right. I've always known my mother was behind it. The longer I waited to confront her, the greater the battle I would face.

Because I was absolutely certain this would end in a battle.

CHAPTER 14

PRESS CONFERENCE, TAKE THREE

One thing you can say about Chief Dullart was that he learned from his mistakes. He was holding his latest press conference at a location where the public couldn't mess up his live shot: the county jail. The seat of Crab County was in an agricultural community several miles inland from Jellyfish Beach, and that's where the jail was.

Attendance was by invitation only. Matt was one of the few journalists allowed in, and he would have to pass through security checkpoints. There would be no one doing squats in a thong or smacking their husband with a scuba flipper at this press conference.

I had no choice but to watch it on TV. The camera shot was too tight to reveal where in the jail complex the conference was taking place, but it appeared to be in an administrative wing.

When I say the shot was tight, it was still wide enough to include the uniformed officers standing behind and on both sides of the chief's podium. It must have been a great honor to be chosen to stand there, square-jawed and glowering with self-importance.

The chief may have once been square jawed when he flanked some previous chief at press conferences, but now he was jowly. His fatty jowls folded over the crisp collar that appeared so tight on his neck, it threatened to cut off the flow of his carotid arteries.

"I'm pleased to announce the arrest of the prime suspect in the recent murders that have been inflicted on the peaceful city of Jellyfish Beach," he said in his southern drawl, strangely high-pitched for a heavy guy like him.

Cameras in burst mode fired off shots like machine guns.

"The suspect's name is Frank Fitzwhizzle, a notorious radical, extremist, lunatic environmental terrorist. He was allegedly working on behalf of a dangerous gang of thugs called Frank's Friends of Florida. He has been charged with first-degree murder, terrorism, using a destructive device for an act of violence, and other offenses. His motive was to punish sportsmen who were taking advantage of nature's bounty in this beautiful low-tax state we call home. We have found more than enough evidence to make these charges stick, so I feel confident to predict that Mr. Fitzwhizzle will receive the maximum penalty under the law. I will now open the floor to a minimal number of questions from the press."

I wasn't surprised that Matt was the first to be called on, since being in-your-face was one of his key personality traits.

"Chief, can you tell us what evidence you found?"

"No."

"Can you tell us what *kind* of evidence? You know, DNA, prints, murder weap—"

"No. Danielle from W-U-S-S TV is next."

"Sir, you're saying you believe the suspect is responsible for all the recent murders, including the explosion on the fishing boat?"

"Yes, we believe so. And, for the record, they're the *only* murders we've had lately in our safe, cozy community."

"He killed the guy who was stealing turtle eggs?" Matt blurted out, not waiting to be called on.

"Yes, we believe so."

"Well, that guy could hardly be considered a sportsman."

"It's not some environmental group's right to kill a poacher. Now, everyone, please wait for me to call on you. George—you go."

"What first alerted you to investigate this suspect?"

"He has a history of eco-terrorism."

"Chaining yourself to a bulldozer is not terrorism!" Matt exclaimed.

The chief's jowls were turning red, and his forehead glistened with sweat. "Stop speaking out of turn, Rosen, or you'll be thrown out of here. As I was saying when you rudely interrupted me, the suspect has a known history, plus we received a legitimate tip from one of his collaborators."

"From whom?" asked Danielle of WUSS.

"I can't divulge that. From a legitimate source."

Matt blurted out, "Isn't the sea-turtle poacher the same guy in the thong bathing suit who disrupted your press conference on the beach?"

The jowls were now a shade of purple.

"Rosen! I will tolerate no one disrespecting me, especially in public. One more time, and you're out of here!"

The sound of a scuffle came from off camera, and the reporters broke into loud murmuring. "Settle down," Chief Dullart demanded. "This press conference will remain orderly, or I'll end it."

The reporters started shouting questions, hoping the loudest ones would be answered. The chief looked like he'd had enough.

"Silence!" he shouted.

The room went instantly quiet.

"That's better," he said. "Anna from W-A-R-P, you're up."

"Thank you, Chief. Can you tell us how your strong leadership and brilliant crime-solving created a breakthrough in this case?"

"Excellent question. Yes, it began with my strong leadership and my vision. I want nothing more than to keep our community safe and thriving. So, I . . . are you guys listening?"

"I smell smoke," someone said off camera.

"Me, too."

"Our community needs someone strong and wise to look up to, and that is my destiny."

An alarm went off.

The chief's jowls and his cheeks turned an even darker purple as he scowled with rage. One of the officers flanking him whispered in his ear.

"No!" the chief shouted. "Let me finish."

The fire sprinklers went off, raining down on the chief and his phalanx of subordinates. The cameras continued to roll.

"Ladies and gentlemen," the chief said. "Do not panic."

A shot was fired in the distance. The crowd was jabbering with panic. Just as the officers on stage huddled together in discussion, a man in an orange jumpsuit ran across the room. Another one followed. Then came a stampede of a dozen prisoners, sprinting across the camera's POV and disappearing.

"Let's exit the room in an orderly fashion," the chief shouted above the alarm.

A jail guard ran into the camera's shot and fired a shotgun. The recoil made him slip on the wet floor, and he fell backward into the chief. They both went down hard.

"Oh, my," I said aloud, and the cats glanced up at me.

Finally, the TV station cut away from the press conference to a shot in their news studio. An anchorman was texting on his phone with his feet on the desk until he realized he was live on camera.

"Chief Dullart is wrapping up the live press conference announcing the arrest of a subject in the recent environmental-related murders. Join us here at five p.m. for the latest on the attempted jailbreak."

"Poor Chief," I said to the cats. "He just can't catch a break."

"Serves him right," Tony said. "What a pompous buffoon."

"You should respect our law enforcement," I scolded. "Even if you're an iguana."

THE NEXT DAY, my phone rang.

"Mindle? Detective Shortle here. It's a mess out there."

"Good morning. I'm fine, thanks. And how are you?"

"Those defilements keep popping up everywhere. I've warned all the houses of worship about the weird altars, and they've been removing them, but it happens at nearly every service. The faith leaders are complaining straight to the chief and the mayor."

"I'm doing all I can. I will place wards at every church, assembly hall, synagogue, and mosque. Even the Hindu temple in the next town."

Working on this problem with Shortle required me to divulge more than I would have liked about my witchy abilities. She hadn't questioned me. She was too desperate to end the problem. And to her, the defilements were about vandalism and the resulting public-relations headaches. She clearly didn't buy the notion that people could lose their souls.

"We've increased our patrols," she said, "but we don't have enough officers to guard every house of worship at every service. And we have no clues of who the perpetrators are. The security footage never shows them. Those altars just magically appear."

I couldn't explain to her about the imp. No talking to the police about supernatural creatures.

"I'll continue to do everything I can," I said.

Finding Angela, however, was my priority. If only I could find a way to do it.

In the meantime, I once again gathered my supernatural "brain trust." The ghost of a wizard who had died 400 years ago and a green iguana. They were the best minds I had.

"Who can tell me how to catch an imp?" I asked.

"Why the heck would you want to do that?" Tony asked. "And where would you keep it? It's not going in the garage with me."

"I'm not going to keep it. I'll catalog it for the Friends of Cryptids and somehow send it far from Jellyfish Beach."

"Catching an imp sounds like something a black-magic sorcerer or a necromancer would do," Don Mateo said. "Not my cup of tea."

My brain trust wasn't living up to its name.

"Has this imp been manifesting in spirit or material form?" Tony asked.

I explained it was physical enough to set up the altars but didn't appear on video and could make itself disappear instantly.

Tony thoughtfully scratched his chin with his claw.

"Can you get a dreamcatcher?"

"I think there's one for sale in the botanica."

"Bring it home, and we'll do the necessary modifications."

The dreamcatcher was Native American and hung on the wall above the crystals in the section of the botanica dedicated to Wicca and witchcraft. I brought it home the next day.

It was an intricately woven net, framed by a circular hoop of polished wood. Groupings of various types of feathers and beads hung from the hoop. A dreamcatcher does exactly what you'd think: catch bad dreams and evil spirits so they don't trouble you.

Somehow, we were going to make it catch a bad little imp.

"It seems awfully fragile," I said.

"The magic you put in it will be strong," Tony said. "Like you."

TONY KNEW as much as I did about the spirituality of the North American indigenous cultures that invented dreamcatchers—

namely, very little. But he was quite familiar with Central American native cultures after being trained there at a camp for familiars.

He said the devices worked great with spirits but weren't designed for demons or sprites that had physical manifestations.

"To catch the imp, you need to attach small pieces of iron to these strings of beads. Then, weave strands of sawgrass into the net, as well as lemongrass."

"Lemongrass? Really?"

"You gotta trust your familiar. Next, paint the hoop with a solution made from salt, egg yolks, three drops of your own blood, and the sap of a mango tree."

"Okay," I said, taking notes.

"After you do that, purify the dreamcatcher in sage smoke for at least an hour."

He looked at my notes. "Write that down. *For at least an hour.*"

"Got it."

"You still got that vial of holy water?"

"Yeah. I should sprinkle it on the dreamcatcher?"

"No, drink it . . . *Of course, you sprinkle it on the dreamcatcher!*"

"Okay, okay. You don't need to be cranky."

"Sorry," my iguana said, "I'm having nicotine withdrawals."

"I told you I have spells to help you quit."

"Whatever. Now, putting the right spells on this is up to you."

"May I make a suggestion, madam?" said Don Mateo's

voice. It startled me because his apparition hadn't appeared visually.

"Yeah. Go ahead."

"Use a fascination spell. You need the imp to be drawn to the complex pattern of the net. He must be lured to it before you can capture him."

"Okay. And I think I'll attach a binding spell that's nine-tenths completed, to be triggered by the proximity of the imp. Once he's in the trap, it will spring shut."

"Brilliant," he said, still without appearing. I had a feeling he didn't want to go imp hunting with me.

Tony had also disappeared. I caught a whiff of cigarette smoke coming from the backyard. I guess I'll have to catch the imp on my own.

Now, the only question was, at which house of worship should I set my trap? I had to be there physically to complete the imp's capture. How would I know where he would be?

I researched church and temple notices online, as well as in *The Jellyfish Beach Journal*. One upcoming event stood out.

Johnny "Bulldoze the Trees" DeFranco would be hosting the baptism of his first grandchild at the same church where Dave, the hedge-fund-manager-turned-lobbyist, had lost his soul. DeFranco was the town's biggest and most ruthless real-estate developer. I was confident the ceremony would have a huge crowd. With so many souls in the church, it would be a tempting target for the imp and the sorceress who controlled him. Namely, my mother.

CHAPTER 15
MONSTERS LIVING LARGE

My crepes and Matt's omelet arrived on our table at our usual café with the ocean view. Matt stuffed his mouth full before I even cut my first bite.

"Not only is Chief Dullart incapable of holding a sane press conference," I began, "but he also seems blind to reality. I'm convinced Frank Fitzwhizzle isn't the murderer, despite whatever alleged evidence was found."

Matt thankfully swallowed his bite before he replied, "The evidence was probably planted."

"By whom?"

"By the folks at NUTS. When you think about it, Frank is a rival. He has the same mission, but he now advocates only peaceful means of protest. That makes NUTS look like the extremist kooks Chief Dullart has been railing against."

"You think they're actually the murderers?"

"It wouldn't surprise me. And it would give them a stronger

reason to frame Frank. I want to dig up more info on them. Are you interested in joining me?"

I shook my head. "Angela is a captive of monsters. How can I do anything other than try to find her?"

"The tasks aren't mutually exclusive, you know. Harriet from NUTS has seen a munuane, and I bet she knows even more than she's letting on."

"I don't want to depend on this Harriet woman to help me find Angela."

"Then what is your plan? Hope that the Friends of Cryptids Society can force the munuane you caught to confess?"

"No. They haven't told me anything, so I'm going to use my magic. The locator spell I know isn't as powerful as Angela's. Mine needs an item from the missing person for it to work." I pulled an envelope from my purse. "Like this."

"What is it?"

"After the vampires and werewolves raided the mansion where the munuane family was staying, I went back inside. It turns out they shed even more than my cats do. I have a clump of their fur, which should be more than enough to make my spell work."

"If you're able to locate them, please don't go there alone."

"Of course not. I would think the Society would help me rescue one of its members."

"I was thinking of me. I want to be with you if you go. Yeah, I'm not much of a bodyguard, but I'd be sick with worry if I wasn't with you."

I smiled and took a bite of my egg and chives crepe. After chewing and swallowing and checking my teeth with my tongue for errant chives, I smiled again.

"That's very sweet of you. You might regret it, though."

I KNELT within a magic circle on my kitchen floor with five tea candles burning—one at each point of a pentagram, each one representing an element. I gathered my energies and drew upon the power of the elements, combining them all together into a force that made my entire body hum.

Then, I drew the energy from the fur I held in my hands—the personal energy of the munuane from which it came.

I chanted the words of the spell, half of which came from languages I didn't understand. Finally, I released the energies, causing a physical sensation akin to expelling my life force.

The glowing orb appeared, levitating at the height of my head. With what little energy I had left, I made a mental connection with the orb.

An image formed in my mind of my own face from the orb's point of view.

"Seek the spirit from which you have been separated," I said to the orb.

And off it flew, quickly passing through the roof of my house and flying too quickly to give me a sense of the visual data I was getting.

The orb slowed its flight. Now, it was soaring above a rare stretch of the Intracoastal Waterway—a small parcel of preserved land covered with mangroves and untouched by development.

The munuanes were living in here? It made sense.

But the orb kept going until it reached luxury townhomes

built next to the mangroves, clustered around a private marina. It passed through the walls of the unit directly adjacent to the mangrove swamp.

The munuane family, minus the one we captured, was sitting around the family room as if they owned the place. Relief flooded my body when I saw Angela sitting on the couch between the father and mother. They were watching the Nature Channel on the television. Angela seemed just as engrossed in the program as her captors were.

Legendary monsters of the wild watching TV? In another expensive home? How had they developed such a taste for luxury and human culture?

It felt wrong, so wrong.

THANKS to the community's unique location, it was easy to find it on a mapping app and get the street address. But now that I'd found it, who would help me raid it? The residents of Seaweed Manor and Squid Tower believed they had fulfilled any obligation they'd had to me and would not take part in another dangerous raid.

Who else could I turn to?

Unfortunately, the Friends of Cryptids Society had more resources for capturing research specimens than they did for rescuing their own members.

"Since Angela is the local enforcer for this area," Mr. Lopez explained when they showed up unexpectedly at my house, "she would normally do the rescuing."

"Obviously, she cannot at the moment," Mrs. Lupis said. "We're bringing in our enforcer from a nearby region."

"You guys seem kind of low on personnel."

"We're a scientific organization," Mr. Lopez said.

"Pseudoscientific, if you believe our detractors," his partner added.

"We have lots of researchers to study monsters. People who can fight with monsters, not so much."

"Harvey from the Gulf Coast Region will meet you at the entrance to the townhome community at midnight. Will you be ready?"

"Ready as ever."

When they left, I called Matt. This time, I couldn't protect him from danger. I needed his help too much.

"I'm taking you up on your offer to come with me to rescue Angela. Can I pick you up at eleven tonight?"

"Um, yeah." He sounded like I had woken him up.

"You said you're not much of a bodyguard, but you'll do, my friend."

I LOOKED up the townhome's street address on the county property appraiser's site. It seemed like a wise move to know the owner of the property we were about to force our way into.

But there wasn't a person's name, only a company name— Mangrove Ventures. It was most likely a holding company that rented out the condo. I briefly wondered how much the munuane family was paying in rent before I realized how ridiculous the thought was. Mangrove Ventures would not accept payment in fish, which was all the ogres could offer.

It was conceivable that the monsters had found the mansion on the beach empty and squatted there. But I doubted they could be that lucky with two consecutive places. Someone was giving the munuanes places to live. Who would do that? Besides, this condo didn't have the same owner as the mansion, Felix Dingledorf.

"How do you find out who owns a holding company?" I asked Matt over the phone, explaining why I was asking.

"You can look up the company under the Florida Division of Corporations and find out who registered it. Often, though, shady people will use aliases to do it."

I kept him on the phone while I found the database on the internet and looked up Mangrove Ventures. When I saw the result, I gasped.

"It says the owner is John Smith," I said. "Obviously fake. But when I search the database using his name, there's a slew of other company names, one of which is Dingledorf Family Holdings. Felix Dingledorf is the owner of the beachfront mansion where the munuanes were living before."

"Felix Dingledorf? The name sounds familiar."

"Affird told me Dingledorf is an alias for a drug lord from Miami. I need your help in breaking into his condo."

"Wonderful," Matt said. "A drug lord's condo. What could go wrong?"

"I broke into his mansion, and the drug lord didn't kill me."

"Not yet. The mansion is probably one of several residences. This condo, though, is a business property."

"Maybe he rents it out for extra income."

"A drug lord needs extra income from a rental condo? He probably uses it to store drug shipments. Or maybe it's a safe house for his assassins. And you want to break into it?"

"We need to rescue Angela," I said as the craziness of my scheme became more apparent.

"Only in Florida would you have a condo occupied by both monsters and drug assassins."

"Your imagination is getting ahead of you. The condo is probably rented by retired people from Queens."

I went on to explain that all we had to do was bust through the door, immobilize the munuanes with magic, and grab Angela.

"We'll be in and out in less than a minute."

Famous last words.

Matt and I arrived at the townhome before midnight. Harvey, from the Society, showed up ten minutes later, stepping out of an old car that was in even worse shape than mine. He was in his forties, balding, of average height, and wearing glasses. He seemed reasonably fit, but wasn't what you would consider hired muscle.

After he, Matt, and I introduced ourselves, I explained the situation. He didn't seem fazed at all that we had to break into a home with five South American ogres inside.

Yes, I was rude, but I asked some direct questions.

"Are you a mage or wizard?"

"Nope."

"A witch?"

He shook his head.

"Then what are your special powers?"

"Special powers? I'm a black belt in taekwondo."

"How nice. You're an enforcer, right?"

He nodded.

"How do you enforce anything against supernatural monsters with taekwondo?"

He laughed. "I guess I've just been lucky. I prefer to be myself and reason with their better nature."

He was not inspiring me with confidence. Maybe this guy was a beginner and has only had to deal with sprites or pixies.

"Okay, I'm going to cast a protection spell around the three of us, so stay together to remain inside the bubble. From a previous run-in with these creatures, I learned my immobility spell works, if I have direct visual contact with them. Keep an eye out if any of them try to hide. And remember, we're trying to save the human. Don't do any martial arts on her."

I pulled a baseball bat from my trunk and handed it to Matt.

"*This*? This is my weapon against ogres?" Matt whined.

"I have magic. Harvey has. . . martial arts. You have a bat. You can't use a firearm—it would cause neighbors to call the police and our goal is to not kill the munuanes. Would you rather have a tennis racquet?"

"Never mind. Your magic better work."

Ideally, magic comes from a place of love. Magic that inflicts harm on others, or acts merely to control them, is corrupt and corrupts the magician—at least in my kind of magic.

Therefore, I wasn't keen on neutralizing the munuane

family with my sleep and immobility spells. But I really had no choice. And having all this pressure on me to perform made it even more difficult. *You* try executing flawless spells with Angela's safety in your hands and Matt whining in your ear.

The orb I had used to locate the family had already been absorbed back into their energy, so I couldn't use it to see what was going on in there. My penetration spell would have to suffice. It enabled me to look into a room as if through a peep-hole in a wall. I explained to Matt and Harvey what I was going to do.

"I know I'm not a witch, but why don't you just look through the window?" Harvey asked, standing at the corner of the building. The condo, being an end unit, had windows along the side facing the mangrove forest. The living room window wasn't covered by blinds, and light poured out into the night. I approached it, crouched, and peered over the sill.

The family and Angela were still watching TV, sitting on the couch and armchairs. They ate cooked fish with their hands, not using plates, creating a mess on the furniture. Monsters don't care about stuff like that. Angela was the only one with a plate in her lap and utensils in her hands.

I had a perfect vantage point. The glass of the window might weaken the immobility spell but would pose no problem for my sleep spell. If I could put them to sleep, I could go around and unlock the front door and, once inside, use the immobility spell to ensure that they were subdued. Matt and Harvey could carry Angela out of the townhome, and I would break the sleep spell on her.

I motioned for my team to stay away from the window and be quiet. Since it wasn't practical to use a magic circle in the carefully manicured strip of lawn, I grasped the power charm in my pocket to give me extra energy as I cast the sleep spell.

It was a simple spell, and within two minutes, the munuanes' eyeless heads slumped to their shoulders and the eyelids on their knees closed. Angela slumped to the side, snoring, as her plate slid from her lap and clattered onto the floor. Everyone slept through the noise.

"Okay. You guys ready?" I whispered. "Matt, you take position outside the porch facing the Intracoastal. Harvey, you come in the front door with me."

I jogged to the front door to use my unlocking spell.

"Oh, no," I whispered. "It's a fancy new electronic lock. This will take a bit longer."

Talk about an understatement. It took nearly ten minutes to unlock the darned thing. Harvey's impatience rose from him like body odor, though I tried to ignore it. I had to remain calm to concentrate.

Finally, the lock clicked, and I pulled the door open. We hurried down the hallway, past the kitchen and into the living room. Everyone in the room was still zonked out, so I began my immobility spell.

"There's only four of them," Harvey whispered. "You said there were six of them, minus the one you captured. So, there should be five here."

The energy I was collecting fizzled out. He was right—there were only four ogres here. The father, who had been sitting in the chair nearest the TV, was missing.

Had he wakened himself from the spell?

I got my answer when a giant figure came pounding down the stairs with a loud roar.

Yes, I admit I screamed. But I quickly began creating a new protection spell around Harvey and me. I had no faith in his martial arts abilities.

Turns out that taekwondo wasn't his superpower. Harvey expanded right in front of my eyes, sprouting thick, dark-brown fur, his clothing splitting at the seams.

Yes, he was a shifter.

A were-bear. Grizzly, to be exact. Once he had fully shifted, he was as large as the munuane father. The ogre didn't bother with his bow and arrow. He simply dove into the grizzly bear. The collision sounded like a thunderclap and shook the walls.

I don't care what kind of ogre you are; you don't want to mess with a grizzly bear. The Harvey-bear recovered from the collision and slammed the munuane's head with his forepaw.

Daddy munuane staggered backward, then pushed forward and shoved the grizzly. Harvey-bear almost fell onto the stairs, but grizzlies are heavy and have a low center of gravity. And, in this case, a human brain. Harvey-bear grabbed the banister and regained his balance. While still upright on his hind legs, he kicked the munuane.

And hit Daddy's left knee and the eye that was on it.

The munuane howled with a cry of such pain that it made the hairs on the back of my neck stand up—a cry unlike that of any mammal on earth.

The eye on the kneecap was bleeding and swollen shut.

I thought the death match would come to its conclusion, but the munuane spun on his heel and rushed into the living room. He went to the sofa and scooped Angela into his arms, rushing like a football running back to the sliding-glass doors facing the water. He smashed through the glass, Angela cradled protectively in his arms.

Matt screamed from outside, and I heard the bonk of the aluminum baseball bat hitting a solid object.

Then came a splash of something very large landing in the Intracoastal Waterway.

And so there I was, the only human among a panting, bloodied grizzly bear and four sleeping South American ogres. The Nature Channel played on the TV, interrupted by a silly commercial for a pet-food delivery service.

Amidst all my shock and dismay, I had the presence of mind to create my immobility spell, keeping the rest of the munuane family in place for the Friends of Cryptids Society.

Then I turned to the grizzly bear, nearly twice my height and five times my weight, who was breathing heavily and salivating.

"Harvey, do you mind shifting back to human? I'm afraid you'll eat my face."

CHAPTER 16
CRYPTIDS IN CAPTIVITY

The moving van arrived so quickly it was uncanny. A half dozen workers wearing overalls with the Friends of Cryptids Society logo wrapped the immobile munuanes in furniture-packing blankets and rolled them upright on hand trucks up a ramp into the moving van.

"When will this spell wear off?" the foreman asked me. "I forgot how long it lasted on the other ogre."

"Four to six hours," I said. "And they might be cranky when they come out of it."

"Thanks for the warning."

The workers were careful to be quiet. Still, I was nervous that a neighbor would wake up and be suspicious of all the activity. So far, no lights had come on in any windows.

I returned to the condo where Mrs. Lupis and Mr. Lopez were waiting.

"Now you have five munuanes. What are you going to do with them?" I asked.

"Study them, of course," Mr. Lopez said. "Full medical exams with blood testing and the works."

"We're observing the behavior of the one we already have in captivity, taking voluminous notes," Mrs. Lupis said. "A linguist is attempting to communicate with him. Our in-house psychic is measuring and categorizing the creature's supernatural energies."

"Pretty thorough. Are you going to keep them in captivity like in a zoo?"

"Heavens no!" they both exclaimed, though Mr. Lopez's exclamation veered into the profane.

"We don't believe cryptids should be in captivity," Mrs. Lupis explained. "We will hold them only until we've gathered enough data."

"And until we determine conclusively that they murdered the humans," Mr. Lopez added. "If not, we'll let them free."

"Right here in South Florida?"

"They migrated here for a reason, most likely because of climate change."

"Or to be closer to the tourist attractions. You never know." Was that humor from Mr. Lopez?

"Has your linguist had any progress in communicating with the captive?"

The two glanced at each other.

"No," Mrs. Lupis said. "Only the basics about wanting food and such. Angela's magic is the most successful means of communicating with monsters."

We stood in silence, thinking about our failure to rescue her.

"Why did the patriarch take Angela with him when he

escaped?" I asked. "I understand he knew he couldn't save his family and had to escape to avoid my spell. But why go to the trouble of taking Angela with him now that he's alone?"

"Her importance as a hostage has become even more acute because we have his entire family," Mr. Lopez said.

Hostage. I let that sink in. When the munuanes first took Angela, I thought it was because that was the kind of thing monsters did. Actually, I feared they would eat her. Now, the munuane father had her as leverage to force us to return his family to him.

"Well, hurry up with your studies and release the munuanes."

"It's not that simple," Mr. Lopez said. "We have no guarantee they will release Angela in return."

"We must continue searching for her and attempt another rescue," Mrs. Lupis said.

While I was thinking about that, Matt called out to me from the master bedroom in the rear, facing the water. He was on his knees beside the bed. The contusion on his forehead from the baseball bat was even more pronounced. The bat *he* was supposed to have been wielding.

"Don't go touching stuff and leaving your fingerprints around," I said.

"I'm not. Look under the bed."

I squatted and lifted the duvet so I could peek.

"Yeah. There's a folded tarp. So what?"

"That's a heavy-duty PVC tarp, completely waterproof. It's often used to protect cargo on sea voyages."

"And?"

"And drug smugglers use it to protect their contraband. I

was thinking about Dingledorf. He probably used this condo as a way station for drugs shipped into the country. Maybe they bring it in through the inlet and transfer it here to boats traveling up the Intracoastal Waterway to other states."

"You believe Dingledorf really is a drug lord?"

"Yep."

"What could he possibly have to do with the munuanes?"

"I have no idea. We need to find out."

I GAVE MATT A RIDE HOME. Before he got out of the car, he leaned over and gave me a reassuring hug. Was it a brotherly hug? Was our relationship turning completely platonic, despite my intentions?

To be honest, I had more important things to worry about. Like Angela. And new doubts about my magic's efficacy. How had the father munuane awoken from my sleep spell? Maybe he hadn't been bewitched in the first place. Did he leave the room before I finished the spell? I was too busy casting it to notice.

I arrived home after 4:00 a.m., needing to get some sleep. But apparently, my cats thought the day was just beginning.

Hoping to sneak into bed, I went into the bathroom and found Bubba sitting on the counter, happy to see me.

"Hey, big guy," I said, petting his head and rubbing his cheeks. The ritual of brushing my teeth was observed by the gray tabby staring at my face with expectation.

I rinsed. "Let's sleep a bit, then I'll feed you. It's too early now."

As I turned to head into the bedroom, he tapped me on the elbow.

Ignore him, I told myself. Get into bed, and he'll go back to sleep. I disrobed in the closet and dropped everything in the hamper. But just before I crawled into bed, the moonlight slipping past the blinds revealed a shape sitting on my pillow.

Brenda. She chirruped as I pulled back the covers and got into bed.

"Just let Mom sleep a couple of hours, and then I'll feed you."

I nudged her from the pillow and sank my face into it.

Then I almost suffocated when she sat upon my head.

"Mmmrph," I said.

"Myrrh," she replied.

There was enough oxygen getting into my squashed nostrils to allow me to survive. That was good enough for me. I began to drift off to sleep.

Bubba meowed from the foot of the bed. I ignored him. With one cat on my ankles and the other on my head, I slowly headed toward dreamland.

"What's a guy gotta do to get a meal around here?" asked a gruff New York accent.

Tony. How had he gotten in from the garage, and why was he in my bedroom? Cats are cute and snuggly; iguanas are not creatures you want near your bed.

"Get out of here," I replied, though my voice was muffled by the cat on my head.

"I got every right to be here. I'm your witch's familiar. We're like partners."

Bubba and Brenda both hissed and growled at him.

"I can tell when I'm not wanted."

"Mm-hmm."

"Guess I'll go eat the flowers in the vase in the foyer."

"Mm-hmm."

Sleep mercifully took me away.

At 6:30 A.M., my phone lying on my bedside table buzzed from a text. I fumbled for it and saw the text was from Matt.

The cats snapped to attention. Finally, it was feeding time!

"Yo! You're back on duty?" called a voice from my bedroom doorway.

The text said that Matt's contact with the police had emailed him the news that forensics determined the explosion on the *Sea Fog* had been caused by a pipe bomb.

"Highly unlikely a munuane fabricated and planted a pipe bomb," he added.

Yeah, the explosion on the boat had always been a piece that didn't fit. It was a stretch to believe a munuane had tampered with a fuel line. Now, it was impossible to believe one was responsible for a pipe bomb.

"Can't you hear my stomach growling?" Tony asked.

I sighed with an unbearable weariness and rose from my bed.

No rest for the witchy.

I HAD NEVER BEEN BAPTIZED. No, it wasn't because of my witchy genes. It was because my adoptive parents weren't particularly religious, attending a Unity church only occasionally. My birth mother was allegedly raised as a Catholic, but she had obviously left the fold big time.

Therefore, I was fascinated as I watched the ritual of baptism. The parents and godparents stood with the priest near the front of the church, DeFranco and his wife hovering behind them. The pews were filled with guests.

I stood in the shadows unnoticed, just inside the door, as if I were an usher. The ceremony was beautiful, but I had to remain focused on the wards I had placed outside, on and around the front steps. Soon, I no longer heard the priest or the responses. It was as if I were outside, listening to the chirping birds, waiting for the imp to show up. That is, if he intended to.

Movement in the church broke my concentration. The priest walked to the baptismal font, followed by the parents, who were holding the baby, godparents, and the rest of the immediate family.

"Do you renounce Satan and all his works? And all his empty promises?" the priest demanded in a booming voice with his hand in the holy water.

That was when—pardon my language—all heck broke out.

A soul-chilling shriek came from just outside, followed by cursing in a high-pitched voice. Something slammed repeatedly against the heavy oaken doors as the family and congregation looked in my direction with horror.

"No worries, folks," I said, holding up my hands. "Continue with the ceremony. I'll take care of this."

I opened the door and slipped out.

The dreamcatcher was zipping around in the air like an enraged hornet. A large burlap sack and a spilled bowl of blood lay on the ground beside the steps. The imp must have gotten caught in the trap as he was about to set up the black-magic altar.

The netting of the dreamcatcher bulged as if it were about to break, but the imp was invisible as he flew in a panic, trying to escape.

I quickly cast a spell to strengthen the binding spell. Then I cast an immobility spell. I was relieved to see it worked on this minor demon. The dreamcatcher dropped to the concrete landing.

"Show yourself, imp!" I commanded.

And there before me appeared a furious imp. He was green, as the witness had reported. He had tiny horns on his vaguely human-shaped head, fangs, a corkscrew tail, and bat-like wings.

"Say cheese!" I snapped several photos of him with my phone for the Society's compendium of cryptids. Technically, a demon such as an imp wasn't a cryptid, but the Society's interests included everything supernatural.

The church door began to open. I immediately sealed it with magic before anyone could see what was going on out here.

Once my spells wore off, the imp could escape to Hell or wherever he lived. But I needed to ensure he didn't return to Jellyfish Beach.

So, I picked up the dreamcatcher—which was surprisingly heavy with the imp in it—and dumped it in the trunk of my car. I headed toward the beach and went north along the shore on Highway A1A.

I pulled into Inlet Park and drove to the seawall right beside the inlet and its strong current. I was amazingly lucky that the tide was going out. Two fishermen were nearby, but most anglers were on the pier atop the jetty, which extended into the ocean at the mouth of the inlet.

As nonchalantly as if I were unloading fishing gear, I pulled the imp from my trunk and carried him to the seawall.

I cast a banishment spell on him.

"Never again shall ye set foot on these shores," I said as I broke the binding and immobility spells. Before he could escape, I dumped him out of the dreamcatcher into the water. The green, horned head bobbed above the surface as the current took him out to sea.

He'd be fine. You can't destroy a demon with drowning. But if my banishment spell worked, we wouldn't have to worry about church defilements again.

Unless my mother found another imp.

I sighed.

CHAPTER 17
I GOT THE KAZOOS, BABY

Some vampires refuse to text. You need to be patient with them. After all, can you imagine what it's like to be hundreds of years old and constantly forced to learn new technologies, slang terms, fashion trends, and the names of the latest hot celebrities? It would be daunting, especially if you were turned late in life. An elderly human might be attached to the cultural ephemera of the 1950s. Imagine if you were stuck in the 1850s—or 1750s?

I had to give Agnes credit. Her late-teens and early adult years were in the fifth century AD. She couldn't get any of the music from back then on her streaming service. But Agnes somehow got by in the modern world. She even texted just as well as a teenager.

Detective Affird was not as adept at texting, but he was okay. He was turned a little more than a year ago when he was in his fifties. I preferred texting him over calling him and

164

hearing his lifeless voice. It sounded that way when he was alive. Now that he was undead, it was even more unnerving.

What can you tell me about Felix Dingledorf? I texted him. *He owns both the mansion we raided and a condo on the Intracoastal. The munuanes were in both of his properties, and the patriarch is still holding my associate captive.*

It took a while for him to answer. And "a while" for a vampire is unbearably long for a human.

I already told you he is a drug lord. I could almost hear the lifeless voice dripping with impatience.

Yes, but what's his real name?

Felix Carrascal.

Thank you. Where is he from originally?

Colombia.

Ah, that made sense. The munuanes are said to be indigenous to the lowland areas of Colombia and Venezuela.

Any chance you can help me speak with him?

I don't know him. I only know about him from working on a case with the DEA. He has a home in Miami and bought the one here in Jellyfish Beach not long ago. I never had a case involving him.

Does he spend more time in Miami or up here?

Don't know. Probably up here.

I guessed that was all I was going to get out of Affird. But then the little pulsing dots appeared on my phone, indicating he was typing. I waited impatiently.

Your reporter friend, Rosen, could ask for an interview. I hear Carrascal is a huge kazoo collector. Rosen could say he's doing a story on it.

I thanked him with profuse emojis. This kind of subterfuge was right up Matt's alley.

Wait, did Affird really write "kazoo collector"? Aren't kazoos those cheap little musical instruments that look like a pipe you hum into, creating a buzzing sound? The kind of instrument used in comedy soundtracks?

I looked up the word just to be sure. Yep, I was right. Why would anyone collect kazoos, especially a wealthy drug lord? I could see him with rare antique violins like a Stradivarius, for instance. Not kazoos. No one collects kazoos, except for eleven-year-old boys, like the one on the street where I grew up who had five of them and formed a kazoo band with his sisters.

I got to the end of the Wikipedia article about kazoos, and there it was: "Colombian-born businessman Felix Carrascal is believed to have the world's largest collection of kazoos, many of which date from the early nineteenth century."

I forwarded the link to Matt, then called him to make my pitch.

"I don't know what's crazier," he said, "that you want me to interview a drug lord or that he's a renowned kazoo collector."

"It's a totally softball interview. Nothing about his business, so it's not risky. Getting him to talk about his passion will soften him up, so we can probe about munuanes."

"What do ogres have to do with kazoos?"

"They're both weird."

"Okay, I'll see if I can reach him and request an interview. Don't get your hopes up, though. International criminals tend to avoid publicity."

It turned out Matt was wrong. He had somehow found an email address that worked, and Carrascal's assistant replied quickly, offering Matt a thirty-minute time slot with the drug lord/kazoo collector.

WE LEARNED that Felix Carrascal owned at least two multi-million-dollar oceanfront mansions, because the one we went to for the interview was not the same one I had raided. This one was even gaudier and more grandiose. After we were buzzed through the wrought-iron gates, we parked on a wide cobblestone driveway behind a fleet of black luxury SUVs.

"Maybe we should have taken your car," Matt said.

We were in his old, beat-up pickup truck. Even the poorest subcontractor doing work on this property would drive a nicer vehicle. Unfortunately, my car was even more embarrassing than Matt's.

"Not a good idea," I said, climbing from the cab. I was dressed in the only outfit I owned that approximated a business suit: a red skirt with a matching blazer. Matt wore jeans fancied up with a tweed sport coat and a narrow blue tie. My high heels weren't handling the cobblestone driveway well. I'm a nurse; I normally only wear shoes that don't hurt after you stand in them for twelve hours—even after I stopped working in hospitals.

Matt rang the bell beside the imposing oaken front doors, as wide and twice as tall as my garage door. It looked like they could withstand the battering ram of a medieval army. They opened, revealing a tiny Latina housekeeper.

"Welcome," she said after Matt introduced us. "Mr. Carrascal is waiting for you in the library."

We followed her down a long hallway modeled after the Palace of Versailles. We passed several rooms until we reached the library at the end. When I was a kid, oceanfront homes were usually funky fishermen's cottages. Not royal palaces. Welcome to the new Florida, where the rich spend their ill-gotten gains. The housekeeper pushed open the double doors.

The two-story-tall library had no books. Instead, the walls were mounted with kazoos, plastic and metal, in multiple colors, and in various shapes representing the evolution of the instrument. I'm talking about two-story-tall walls with rows and rows of mounted kazoos. There was even a wheeled library ladder so you could examine them up close.

This must be the world's epicenter of kazoos. Little had I known that humble Jellyfish Beach possessed this honor.

At the center of the room stood a rotund man wearing tennis whites. He had a gray beard, a shock of fake-looking black hair, and a kazoo between his lips.

"Hail to the Chief" buzzed from the kazoo.

Matt and I stood dumbstruck.

Carrascal pulled the kazoo from his mouth and smiled. "Welcome to my collection! I am so proud to show it to you." His Colombian accent was cultured and slight.

Matt and I introduced ourselves, and we all shook hands. Carrascal offered us seats in front of a fireplace where a fire roared, despite a temperature outside in the seventies.

I noticed a man standing in the corner of the room, near a row of gold-plated kazoos. Also dressed in tennis whites, he looked like the stone-cold killer you'd expect to see at a drug lord's home, unlike his jovial boss. Sweat formed in the center of my back. Was it the heat of the fire, or the vulture-like eyes staring at me?

"Thank you for having us, sir," Matt said, taking his narrow reporter's notebook from his back pocket. Matt usually recorded audio, too, during his interviews. He started to take his phone out, but hesitated. Drug lords rarely enjoy being recorded, for obvious reasons. "When did you begin collecting kazoos?"

"When I was a child, still living in Colombia in a poor fishing village, a traveling merchant showed up one day. The adults hoped he brought medicine, or batteries for our radios, or parts for our boats. No, he showed up with crates full of kazoos. And we children were delighted! A magical instrument that anyone lacking musical skills could make songs with. I bought one, a little piece of tin with a vibrating membrane that said, 'Made in the USA.' It was my inspiration to move here and to be the business success that I am today."

A kazoo drove him to become a murderous drug lord? I could believe that.

"When I first visited Miami as a young man," he continued, "I thought I would find people playing kazoos at every street corner. But no, I did not. They played guitars; they played trumpets. They played salsa and merengue. But no one there played music on the kazoo. That made me even more determined to seek out this wondrous instrument."

Matt scribbled away on his pad, seemingly unaffected by the overwhelming emotion his subject was experiencing.

"I did research. I traveled to Georgia, where it is said the kazoo was born, and to Louisiana where it was common. All the way north to the Catskills, to the vaudeville shows and the kazoo museums, I went. In doing so, I discovered the rich heritage of these divine instruments. And I bought them at insanely low prices. Who would sell their cherished kazoo at such a cheap price? Over here," he strolled past his bodyguard and pointed to the wall, "is one of the first kazoos manufactured in the United States, produced before the Civil War. My most treasured—"

A hideous scream came from a nearby room. The bodyguard raced through the door and closed it behind him.

"Made of simple tin and wax paper, it is priceless. Did you know even the serious classical composer and conductor Leonard Bernstein wrote a mass featuring the kazoo? Listen."

With great seriousness, Carrascal played a complex classical melody on the same kazoo he had used when we first arrived. However, it was difficult to imagine this buzzing sound ringing out in a symphony hall.

"Please don't kill me!" cried a man in a nearby room—the same voice we had heard screaming. You'd think a mansion like this would have better sound insulation.

The bodyguard returned to the room and looked at Carrascal, who nodded subtly while still playing. The bodyguard slipped out the door again.

"Your house could be a public museum of kazoos," I said when Carrascal finished his piece.

"The world's preeminent museum of kazoos," Matt added.

Carrascal nodded solemnly. "Yes, I have thought the same. But this is not a good location for a public museum. I would put it in one of my properties on the mainland. However, I could not bear to be separated from my beloved collection."

"You could always visit it, day or night," I said.

"I promise you, I will pay—" the voice screamed before a loud bang rang out.

The bodyguard slipped back into the room and resumed his station beneath a wall of nineteenth-century kazoos.

"The museum shall be my legacy to this community. To this country. But it is not yet time for me to live without my darlings in my home."

Carrascal gazed at the walls of kazoos, thousands of them, rows upon rows mounted from eye level to several yards above. Tears appeared in his eyes.

"You said you're from eastern Colombia?" I asked.

He nodded while trying to contain his emotion.

"Have you ever heard of a creature called the munuane?"

"Of course. The grandfather of the fishes. A legend I heard about as a child."

"Do you believe the creature actually exists?"

After a while, Carrascal pulled his gaze from the kazoos and looked at me, as if he had just noticed I was here.

"The munuane? Why would it not be real? Legends are always based upon kernels of truth, are they not?"

They are literally real, I wanted to say. But didn't dare to do so. How could I discover if Carrascal knew munuanes had been in his properties?

"Are there any munuanes in Florida?" Matt asked.

"It would be nice if there were. Wouldn't it?"

"I NEVER THOUGHT that kazoos could be so inspiring," Matt said, wiping a tear from his eye as he drove up A1A away from the mansion. "You don't need lessons to play one. But with proper instruction, I bet a guy like me could make it to Carnegie Hall."

"I can't tell if Carrascal knows about the munuanes in Jellyfish Beach. He must, though. Right? It's too much of a coincidence that they would break into two of his properties."

"Yeah. But I'm sure other people have access to the keys and could have sent the munuanes to the two homes without Carrascal knowing."

"Why would anyone want to protect them? Is Carrascal that sentimental about his homeland that he would protect monsters from there?"

"He seemed to be cool with them. Oh, no." Matt was looking in his rearview mirror.

"What?"

"We're being followed."

"How can you tell? This is a two-lane road with no passing."

"That red car has been behind us since we left the mansion."

"Pull into the beach parking up there," I said.

Matt turned into the sandy lot.

"No one followed us," I said.

"The red car stopped on the shoulder just past the entrance."

"Do you think it's Carrascal's goons?"

"It's not one of the giant black SUVs that were parked in front of his place. Doesn't mean it's not his people. I'd better drive straight to the newsroom, in case they're checking if we're legit."

Matt turned his truck around and exited the parking lot. When he passed the red, generic American-built sedan, he peered across me into the car.

"A man and a woman. They look like cops to me," he said.

He turned at the next light, and we went across the bridge over the Intracoastal. We made our way west into downtown Jellyfish Beach, Matt glancing at his mirror often enough that I worried he was going to rear-end the car in front of us.

"They're still following us—two cars back."

We arrived at *The Jellyfish Beach Journal*, a large building in a light-industrial neighborhood that was being gentrified. The *Journal* used to have its printing press onsite, but they closed it down and farmed out the printing of the paper editions they still put out—of which there weren't very many. Digital subscriptions were keeping the business afloat.

Folks, support your local newspaper. You'll never know what's going on in your hometown if you only get your news from Crazy Uncle Fred's posts on social media. Also, I don't want Matt to get laid off and move away in search of a job. His other skills—surfing and fishing—don't attract employment offers.

Matt pulled into a shady spot beneath a massive banyan tree, its roots cracking through the asphalt.

The red car pulled in right next to us, so close that Matt wouldn't be able to open his door. The car's passenger window went down, and an African American male signaled for Matt to lower his.

"You're Matt Rosen," the man said.

Matt nodded. "I know."

"We're from the DEA." The man flashed a badge for the Drug Enforcement Agency. "Why were you visiting Felix Carrascal?"

"We were interviewing him."

"Why? We don't want you interfering with our investigation."

"It was for a feature story. Mr. Carrascal is a world-famous collector of kazoos."

"Don't get wise with me."

"I'm serious. Kazoos. You know what they are?"

"Yes, I know what they are! I had one when I was eight. Don't pretend you don't know who Carrascal is."

"We do know. But I'm not working on a story about his drug trafficking. Honestly, it's about kazoos."

"I don't understand why he even agreed to meet with you. He tries to stay under the radar."

"He's really passionate about kazoos."

"Overly passionate," I said.

The agent shook his head. "He's crazy."

"No," I said. "He's a kazoo virtuoso."

"Why are you being so possessive of Carrascal?" Matt asked the agent. "Getting ready to bust him?"

"You know I can't tell you that."

"Are you expecting a big shipment coming in?"

"Knock it off, Mr. Rosen. I'm going to warn you now, and this is the only warning you'll get. If you get in our way, we will arrest you for obstructing an investigation. Understand?"

"Absolutely."

"Have a nice day." The agent's window rose, and they drove away, their side-view mirror clipping Matt's side-view mirror, which looked like it had already been clipped more than once before.

CHAPTER 18
MAKING WAVES

"The DEA agents were very helpful," Matt said.

"Helpful?"

"They reinforced my theory that Carrascal is running drugs through Jellyfish Beach. That tarp I found in the condo was not a one-off. I was under the impression that his shipments came into the Miami area. Originally, I thought that was why he bought homes up here—to live in a quiet place far from his drug runners."

"Instead, he's expanding his operation up here."

"Exactly," he said. "The drugs probably go to the Bahamas from South America, then come to Florida on smaller boats. Lots of fishermen cross back and forth between here and the Bahamas. You spread out your shipment across several boats. Each one holds a small enough cargo that it's easy to conceal."

"Do you think the pipe bomb aboard the *Sea Fog* had anything to do with this?" I asked.

"It sounds like something drug runners would do. Maybe the *Sea Fog* was competing with them."

"Or the *Sea Fog's* captain saw suspicious boats coming over and threatened to report them. Now that I think about it, many pieces are falling into place. The fisherman who was drowned in his cooler at the boat ramp—he might have witnessed a drug shipment coming in. And whoever shot at Rivas's boat was more likely to be a drug runner than a munuane. I think it's time to visit the marina."

"Agreed. Let's go inside and do some homework first."

I followed Matt into the small, cluttered newsroom. Only two other reporters were there. They ignored us, one busy on his phone, the other tapping away on his keyboard.

Matt's desk had piles of news clippings and surfing magazines. A book about witchcraft caught my eye. I pointed to it with raised eyebrows.

"Just trying to get some insight on you, my dear," he said.

That gave me a warm feeling inside.

"I'll search the archives for any articles on Carrascal if you'll search the internet for the name of the captain of the *Sea Fog*. Also, that guy who rents the PWCs—I want to talk to him again."

I tapped on my phone while Matt worked on his computer.

"There's nothing recent about Carrascal," he said. "And nothing that took place in Jellyfish Beach."

"The captain and owner of the *Sea Fog* is Bill Tendrix," I said. "The name of that rental place is Wave Action, but there's no information about who owns it."

"Okay, thanks." He typed away. "Let me see . . . an article about the business opening. Wait—here's something about the missing customer. It says the Marine Patrol found him. Guy named Jimmy Minster. He simply abandoned the watercraft, claiming he received a head injury. The Coast Guard is considering charging him for the cost of their search."

"Ouch!"

"Yeah. I think we should talk to him, although it may be a waste of time. Okay, here's a piece on Bill Tendrix. Busted for drug possession. Two grams of cocaine. Got a fine and probation. Nothing here about smuggling, but he's no choirboy."

WE ARRIVED at the marina when the morning charter boats were still out, except for a dive boat that was just departing. Its long, open stern was filled with divers sitting on benches beside their tanks. As the boat chugged on its way to the nearby reefs, Matt and I stopped by the office of the personal-water-craft rentals.

"Hey, I know you!" the skinny guy with the blond dread-locks said.

"Yes, you do. We stopped by here before. But we don't know your name. I'm Missy and this is Matt."

"I'm Boswell, but my friends call me Boz."

"Boz, we want to ask you about Jimmy Minster, the guy who went missing and never returned his watercraft. Do you still have his deposit?"

"Funny you ask. He came by the other day to settle his charges. Man, he sure was complaining about the Coast Guard."

"Did he say why he abandoned his rental?"

"He said he was attacked by a monster." Boz laughed heartily. "I think the dude was drunk, fell off the watercraft, and swam to shore. Never bothered to call us about the machine."

Matt and I exchanged looks.

"Do you have his address?" Matt asked.

"I'm not supposed to, you know, give it out."

Matt handed him a twenty. "I can find it in public records. But I was hoping you'd save me the bother."

Boz pocketed the money and pulled up a record on his computer. He read aloud a Jellyfish Beach address.

"Thank you," I said. "Let us know if any other customers claim to have seen a monster." Handing him my botanica business card, I added, "And get twenty percent off anything in the store."

He stared at the card uncomprehendingly, afraid to ask what a botanica was.

We stepped outside, and Matt glanced at his watch.

"We have some time before the *Sea Fog* returns. Let's see if Mr. Minster is home."

Jellyfish Beach was founded in the late 1800s by farmers and fishermen who settled where downtown now sits, on the bank of the Intracoastal Waterway. With the ocean serving as a boundary to the east, the town grew to the north and south. With other towns springing up along the waterway, the only abundant land was to the west, where the pioneers' farms used to be. Like the rings of a tree, the further out from the core you went, the more recent the suburban sprawl was.

We drove to the west of downtown, arriving in a middle-class suburban neighborhood that looked like it had been built in the sixties. Minster's one-story home was old and faded. His driveway had a car parked in it, hopefully his. We went to the door and rang the bell.

The young man who answered carried a tall can of beer, though it was before noon. His hair was mussed and his face unshaven.

"Are you Mr. Minster?" I asked.

"You mean my dad or me?"

"Jimmy Minster," Matt said.

"We're both Jimmies. This is my dad's house, so you're probably looking for him. He's at work."

He tried to close the door, but Matt blocked it.

"No, we're looking for you, Jimmy. You recently had an incident with a personal watercraft."

Matt showed his reporter ID.

"Oh. I don't really want to talk about that."

"Jimmy, we believe your story about the monster," I said.

"You do?"

"We've seen it ourselves. That's why we want to talk to you."

"Really?" He scratched his head. "Wanna come in and have a beer?"

We followed him into the living room, which appeared to have the same furniture from when the house was built in the sixties. The exception was the large-screen TV with a paused video game. We turned down the offer of beers as Jimmy plopped himself down on a recliner facing the TV.

"The monster attack really messed me up," he said, taking a deep swig from his can. "Haven't been able to work since then."

"Because of physical injuries?" I asked.

"No. I think I have that post-traumatic thing, whatever you call it."

"Post-Traumatic Stress Disorder," I offered.

"Yeah." He took another deep drink.

"Can you tell us what happened?" asked Matt.

"I was cruising around Beer Can Island and saw a bunch of manatees. I thought that was cool. Figured I'd try to herd them like cows. Bumped into a couple of them." He laughed. "Then, I got bored and stopped at the island to take a leak in the trees. That's when I saw it."

"The monster?"

"Yeah. Freaking huge, hairy thing. It didn't seem to have any eyes. Came running at me, making noises like it was trying to talk. It had a paddle, the kind you use for paddle boards, and it swung it at me. That's the last thing I remember. I woke up later with my head hurting like heck and blood everywhere. My Jet Ski had been pushed off the beach and I didn't know where it was, so I swam to shore."

He gulped the last of his can, crushed it in his hand, and belched.

"You know what freaks me out the most? The last thing I remember seeing was his eyes. On his knees. The monster had eyes on his knees."

"Was it a male?" I asked.

"Yeah. I could tell, even with all his fur."

"Did you ever consider that the monster was punishing you for harassing the manatees?" Matt asked.

"What? That would be crazy, right? I mean, why? Do you think so?" He seemed to consider it. "Maybe I shouldn't harass them anymore."

"Maybe you shouldn't," I said.

When we drove away, Matt said, "It sounds like when I was attacked on the beach. When I didn't release the snook."

"It sure does."

"I'm confused. Every time we decide the killings weren't done by the munuanes, we find out about them causing trouble."

"I think we're conflating two different kinds of attacks," I said. "The munuanes are punishing people who harm water creatures—like you and Jimmy. I believe the murders were committed by humans. Probably involving drug smuggling."

"Yeah, that's where the evidence is leading. Except the gator hunters don't quite fit in. They were far from the ocean and Intracoastal where the smuggling would be."

"Maybe there's a smuggling route through the swamps."

"Or maybe the munuane did kill those two guys."

We thought about it in silence until we returned to the marina. The *Sea Fog* was docked. The repairs had been fast and thorough, so I could see little evidence of the bomb blast aside from a missing door and window on the wheelhouse. Passengers disembarked while the two mates cleaned their catches on a nearby table. The undesirable parts of the fish were swept into the water below, where crabs and other bottom feeders would make short work of them.

I noticed that Rivas's boat wasn't in his slip. Presumably, he was still out fishing.

Captain Tendrix walked down the gangway and into a small hut that served as an office. We followed. He looked up at us from behind a desk, his face tanned and creased from decades in the sun, his blond hair turned white, his frame large and menacing.

"You two again? I'm hoping you're going fishing with us this time. We leave in an hour for the afternoon trip."

"Sorry," Matt said. "More questions."

"I have a lot to do before we set out."

"I know. I'll keep this short. Forgive me for asking stuff the police already asked, but do you have anyone you suspect in planting the bomb?"

His eyes narrowed. "The police did ask that. The answer is no."

"During your charters, have you ever observed anything suspicious, like a boat transferring cargo to another boat?"

"Cargo?"

"I'm thinking of drugs."

"We drift along the reefs close enough you can see us from shore. Any activity you're talking about would take place far out at sea."

"Well, have you seen any suspicious boats coming in or out of the inlet?"

"Are you implying drug traffickers planted the bomb on my boat?" He looked at both of us, and we nodded.

"I have nothing to do with those people."

"We believe you," I said. "But maybe you witnessed something, and they wanted to send you a warning to keep quiet."

"Or to take you out completely," Matt added. "Could the bomb have sunk your boat?"

"I doubt it. The bomb was planted inside the wheelhouse. It was meant for me. I just happened to be on deck at the time, helping the mates with a kingfish that tangled a bunch of lines. Otherwise, I'd be dead."

So, the bomb was much more than a warning.

"Wow," Matt said. "You can see why it looks like drug runners did it."

"I don't know why those guys would want to kill me, unless, like you said, they think I saw something I didn't see."

Was he telling the truth? He could be afraid to talk about the traffickers, even if they were responsible.

I glanced out the window. Rivas still hadn't returned. His routine seemed to be to fish early and return in time to get his catch to the fish markets. He should have been back before now.

"Why isn't Captain Rivas's boat here?" I asked.

Tendrix shrugged. "How should I know?"

"You see him every day. Is his boat being repaired?"

"Not that I know of." He clearly did not want to talk about Rivas.

Rivas had admitted to knowing about the munuanes. So had Carrascal. In fact, they both were from the region the munuanes were from. Did the two men know each other?

"Do you suspect Captain Rivas is involved in drug running?"

"I wouldn't know," he replied to me angrily. "Here at the marina, we look out after each other and our boats. We don't accuse each other of crimes."

He didn't say it like he believed Rivas was innocent, though. He simply didn't want to talk about it—didn't want us outsiders involved.

"Thanks for your help," Matt said, handing two of his business cards to Tendrix. "Please contact me if you get any ideas about who tried to kill you. I'm sure that's top-of-mind for you. Right? I mean, if someone tried to blow me up, I'd be constantly wondering who it was. And give one of these to Rivas when you see him, if you don't mind. Tell him I want to speak with him."

Tendrix nodded with a stony expression, but I wouldn't be surprised if he threw away the cards the moment we walked out.

When we got into Matt's truck, I explained my recent thoughts about Rivas.

"It's too much of a coincidence that two men from the same region as the munuane are living here in Jellyfish Beach," I said. "They must know each other. I want to find out if Rivas put up the munuanes in Carrascal's homes to keep them safe."

"Or if Rivas is running drugs for him. Taking them to shore from a larger boat."

"If he is, he must be on the DEA's radar."

"Yeah, but as you could see, I don't have a good relationship with anyone at the agency. I'm more of a local reporter—not so tight with the feds."

"Well, Rivas must be on the Jellyfish Beach Police's radar. Can you find out what they have on him?"

"Um, well, maybe. Maybe not."

"What's the problem? You've been a reporter here for years."

"Detective Affird, as much as he despised me, was a good source. But your friends at Squid Tower turned him into a vampire, and now he's retired. I have a few other sources I've known for years, but Dullart has clamped down to prevent leaks. He treats the news media like we're enemies. It's hard to get my sources to talk anymore."

"If the chief knew how to give a news conference without embarrassing himself, he wouldn't hate the media."

"There's nothing I can do for now. I'm dealing with constant hostility at the Jellyfish Beach Police Department."

"Then we need to find another way to connect Rivas with Carrascal."

"Even if we discover Rivas was the one who put the munuanes in Carrascal's homes, how does that help us solve the murders?" Matt asked, frustrated with me.

"It doesn't. But if we confirm that he's involved with Carrascal, who also knows of the munuanes, we can tell him we know he's the one putting up the munuanes in Carrascal's houses and demand that he let us know where Angela is. That's my first priority."

"So you want to confront a guy who might be the murderer to ask him if he knows where Angela is?"

"Yes! We can also find out if he killed the people who witnessed his drug runs and alert the DEA guys."

"We might not know for sure unless he comes to kill us."

CHAPTER 19
ENVIRONMENTAL HAZARD

"You know, I'm underutilized here," Tony said from a shelf above me as I mixed a foul-smelling potion on the garage workbench. The stinky, flammable, or paint-damaging ingredients were mixed out here, rather than in my kitchen.

"What do you mean?" I wasn't really paying attention to him, concentrating on getting the right amount of skunk oil into the eyedropper.

"You haven't let me help you with your magic for a while. I have all sorts of talents you don't even know about. I feel unappreciated here."

"I'm sorry, Tony. I've never had a familiar before. Magic has always been a solitary activity for me. You're right—I don't know all your capabilities."

"That's for sure."

"Perhaps that's because you've never spelled them out for me."

"I don't like to brag."

"You seem like the kind of iguana who does."

"Remember when I discovered the existence of a new supernatural entity in Jellyfish Beach?"

"I sure do. That was very helpful. Even though you couldn't identify what it was."

"Hey, I'm a familiar, not a witch. You need to do the groundwork."

"Yeah, after searching for a strange creature—thinking it might even be a microorganism—I found out it was a psychic vampire. Walt Whitman, in fact."

"But I set you on the right trail."

"I wish you could help me find Angela."

"Witches and mages aren't technically supernatural creatures, even if they have the magic gene in them. I can only locate them when they're casting spells and putting out magical energy into the atmosphere. Which brings me to the point at hand."

"Yes, it would be nice if you got to the point."

"There's another witch practicing magic in Jellyfish Beach."

"There is?"

I was surprised because Angela and I were the only true witches, or mages, locally. There were plenty of hobbyists who tinkered with the craft and occasionally produced mild magic. Many were my customers at the botanica. There was also Tim Tissy, AKA Lord Arseton, who borrowed power from a demon. And throughout Crab County, a dozen or so witches plied their trade.

But in Jellyfish Beach, Angela and I were the only shows in

town. Not being a member of a coven was one reason my magic didn't fully develop until I reached middle age.

"Who is it?" I asked.

"Jeez, you know I can't learn specifics like that. See, you're always finding ways to chip away at my self-confidence."

"Not my intention at all. Besides, you seem pretty confident for an iguana."

"I lived in New York with my previous magician. You gotta have a thick skin in the Bronx."

"So, why don't you tell me what you know about this witch?"

"It's a woman. And by the energy she's releasing, I'd wager she's a water witch."

"Very impressive."

"I am, aren't I?"

"You're not so insecure, after all. Tell me, what kinds of spells is she casting?"

Tony stewed for a moment. "You really do know how to undermine my pride."

"What are you talking about? I just want to know what the witch is doing with her magic. Your skin isn't as thick as you say it is."

"I can sense her energy and the element it comes from. Isn't that good enough?"

"Don't be snippy. I don't know the extent of your talents."

"But you know I'm not talented enough."

"Will you stop? You're such an aggrieved iguana."

"For good reason. I'm forced to live in a garage, for Pete's sake."

I ignored his whining. My cats decreed that the iguana

couldn't live in their house, so my perfectly comfortable one-car garage would have to suffice.

"Can you tell me where you're sensing the magic?" I asked.

"West of town. Far west. In addition to the magic, I'm sensing a disruption of the natural equilibrium."

"Can you tell me what that means?"

"It means someone is destroying the environment. Like a developer."

I saw everything now with perfect clarity. The witch was using magic to stop the developer. If my theory was correct, the witch might be a member of NUTS or Frank's Friends of Florida. However, Frank's group seemed to be dormant, especially since Frank had been arrested.

I didn't want to get involved in this. But when you practice magic, you are morally obligated to avoid malignant spells and to ensure no one else uses them, either. And, especially, not to use black magic. Fortunately, this sounded like normal elemental magic—white magic, in other words.

Still, it would be prudent for me to investigate the unspecified witch.

IT DIDN'T TAKE me long to come up with a good guess of where the magic was taking place. All I had to do was open the next morning's edition of *The Jellyfish Beach Journal*.

A full-page ad heralded the soon-to-be-built community of "Savanna Trace, a luxury 55+ active-lifestyle community." The ad featured color illustrations of a great blue heron gliding over grasslands and renderings of the different models of homes that would replace the herons and the grasslands. A sales center had opened on the property. I told Luisa I would be late coming in today, and I headed west on Jellyfish Beach Boulevard, leaving the city limits and continuing until the road's name changed to a now-defunct brand of oranges.

I was in an area that used to have citrus groves until subdivisions replaced them. Going further west, the road used to be unpaved at this point, but now was shiny new asphalt. I was in a land of savannas—grassy wetlands—bordered by a forest of slash pine and palmettos.

And I didn't need to be a witch's familiar to sense the magic permeating the air.

Ahead was a huge sign for Savanna Trace, and just past it, a double-wide trailer that served as the sales center. I parked and went inside.

"Heavens, you are much too young to live in a fifty-five-plus community, my dear."

It was a thin man with hair dyed black and a pink blazer.

"Are you looking for a home for your parents?"

"You read my mind," I lied.

"How many bedrooms do they desire? We have five different floor plans with up to four thousand square feet of living space. They each have a chef's kitchen with granite countertops, volume ceilings—"

"Can I just have a brochure to bring to my folks?"

"Yes, of course." He handed me a thick, expensively printed folder.

"The sign says the community is supposed to open next month?"

"Well, as you can see, we've only begun breaking ground."

"Construction delays?"

"Nothing to be concerned about."

"Mechanical problems? Workers becoming ill? Things like that?"

He looked at me strangely. "Why would you ask that? Our construction company is over-extended. Too many projects going on at the same time."

"Have you had any problems with environmental groups?"

"Developers always do. But I haven't witnessed any protests here."

"That's good news." I put on my biggest fake smile. "Thank you for the brochure. I'll bring my parents with me next time."

A luxury SUV had parked next to my junker, and an elderly married couple walked into the sales center, stealing the salesman's attention and giving me an opportunity to walk upon the small section of grasslands that had been cleared.

A large yellow excavator sat beside stacks of concrete pipes. Magic lingered at the site like the smoke aroma after a long-extinguished fire. I sensed Tony was correct—the magic came from a water witch. It didn't mean that her spells involved water, only that the element of water gave the witch extra energy to strengthen her internal energies. It made sense, I guess, that a water witch would want to protect wetlands. I used all five elements myself, but I was unusual that way.

I strolled around the cleared land, opening all my senses—especially the witchy ones—trying to figure out what spells were at work here.

The yellow excavator loomed above me, its long arm angling upward to its elbow, then extending down to the ground where it rested on its massive claw. The cab was above the tank-like treads. Metal steps enabled me to climb up and sit on the small seat.

That's when I smelled the ozone and sensed the electrical field. The spell the witch used had fried the electrical system of the machinery. Simple and completely untraceable by modern forensics.

I climbed down to the ground. But there was something else—additional magic I couldn't quite place.

Except that I felt the presence of evil.

The magic that killed the excavator's engine was regular, neutral power. This other magic I sensed was different. It was meant to harm humans, such as the construction workers.

It was black magic. A negative force, black magic doesn't use elemental energy. Instead, it draws upon the vacuum of nothingness in the universe, the antithesis of existence. It was all about destruction, death, and utter bleakness. Black magic also employs demons to do its heavy lifting, which makes the magician indebted to the demon.

I knew of only two people involved with black magic. Lord Arseton was enthralled to a demon Arseton incorrectly believed was an angel. I didn't think he knew much magic himself; the demon did all of that for him.

The other black-magic practitioner I knew was my mother. She, of course, was already my primary suspect for the defilements of the houses of worship. I desperately hoped she wasn't up to even more evil acts.

She made a living by selling her services to the highest bidder. I seriously doubted an environmental group could afford her, especially one on the fringe like NUTS. But a group on the fringe would be more likely to turn to black magic than a conventional organization.

It was possible that NUTS had a black-magic sorcerer of their own. It was time to find Harriet, the leader of NUTS, to find out if she was involved in black magic. And to learn if she was responsible for the murders Frank Fitzwhizzle had been charged with.

"I want to find Harriet from NUTS and interview her," I said to Matt over the din of the bar.

We were in the Ripped Tide, a dive bar popular with the surfers and assorted low lifes of Jellyfish Beach. It was one of Matt's favorite spots. Personally, I tried to avoid entering the bathroom at all costs. It was that kind of place.

"You think NUTS was involved in the murders?" Matt asked.

"In her emails, Harriet tried a little too hard to pin the blame on the munuane. Also, I found evidence that magic was used to delay the construction of a development in sensitive lands west of town. I want to know if Harriet, or someone else in the group, is a witch."

"Excuse me for saying so, but you seem angry about it."

His saying so made me angrier.

"Yeah, I felt a trace of black magic. Anyone using black magic around here needs to be stopped."

"And you're wondering if your mother is involved?"

Very perceptive of him, but it made me madder.

"Right. And she'd better not be. After everything I went through with her. Tell me, how can we find Harriet?"

Matt scratched his beard and took a swig from his bottle of beer. I, too, drank straight from the bottle, unwilling to put this establishment's glassware anywhere near my lips. I'm not much of a beer drinker, but I wouldn't even think about ordering wine here.

"I can email her and ask again for an in-person interview."

"She'll just say no like she did before. We need to track her down and catch her unaware."

Matt nodded. "We can find members of Frank's Friends of Florida and ask if they know her."

"I don't know if his organization even exists anymore. But that gives me an idea. If she's such a fervent environmentalist, she'll be involved in many advocacy projects. She's probably a member of groups like the Sierra Club and other Florida non-profits. We can check their membership directories for Harriets, and if we're lucky, we'll find her."

"If Harriet is her real name."

"Yeah." I felt slightly deflated. "That could be a problem. I'm not going to worry about it now, though. Let's start searching. Do you have your laptop with you?" I nodded at his shoulder bag.

"I always do. Unless I'm surfing or fishing."

"Bring it to my place. I'll get on my computer, and you on yours, and we'll pound the pavement of the internet until we find something."

"It's not often a woman asks me to her place to Google with her."

IT TURNED out my idea wasn't as easy as I had thought. The environmental groups don't have their membership directories online for anyone to see, for obvious privacy reasons.

"I'm a member of the Sea Turtle Society," Matt said. "Let's see if we members can access our directory. Well, if I can remember my password."

Twenty minutes and a lot of cursing later, Matt successfully logged on.

"Awesome! Here's the directory . . . Oh, but I don't see any Harriets."

As a member of the Nature Club, I logged on and scoured the site, but couldn't see any listings of members. All the members of the leadership and the staff were listed, but there was no Harriet.

"Do you think she would be on the staff of another organization?" I asked.

"It's conceivable. I doubt NUTS can afford to pay her a salary, so she has to earn money somehow. Of course, her real job could be anything. She could be a professional roller-derby player for all we know."

"Highly probable," I said. "Well, before I give up in despair, I'll search for the leadership and staff of every environmental group I can dig up. You search the internet and news sites for the name 'Harriet' coupled with relevant search terms, such as 'environment' and 'activist.' Okay?"

"If you fuel me with beer."

I went to the kitchen to grab a beer from the supply I keep for his visits and poured myself a glass of wine.

We sat next to each other on the couch, clicking away on our keyboards, while the cats watched us from atop the furniture.

"Music?" I asked.

"Sure."

This was beginning to feel like a date. As Latin music pulsed softly in the background, I noticed we were sitting closer together than before. No, it wasn't the result of magic. It was accidental. But then I got an idea.

And cast a quick, simple spell.

Almost imperceptibly, our butts magically slid closer to the center of the sofa and to each other.

Matt was too busy clicking away, but I could feel his body heat now.

Another imperceptible slide. Now our hips and shoulders touched ever so slightly.

Matt's clicking slowed down. So did mine.

Matt turned to me, confused. "How did we—"

"It doesn't matter."

He leaned in, his face almost touching mine.

"This is supposed to be a working session," he murmured.

"We're searching."

"I've already found what I'm looking for."

His lips brushed against mine.

Then, hissing and growling filled the room.

Brenda and Bubba stood on a chair and table staring with indignation at Tony, who had wandered into the room.

"Am I breaking up a party?" he asked. "I only wanted to hang out where everyone else is. It's lonely out in the garage."

Matt and I returned to clicking on our keyboards. It's one

196

thing to make out in front of cats. But doing so in front of an animal who talked just seemed too weird.

"Don't mind me," Tony said. "I'm chillin'."

"Mind if I get another beer?" Matt asked.

"Go right ahead."

When he returned from the kitchen with his beer, he sat two inches further from me than before.

"Nice choice of music," Tony said. "Hey, you got any flowers I can snack on?"

Why couldn't my witch's familiar be a cat or dog? Why a lizard?

"Hmm. Here's a Harriet Chase," Matt said. "Arrested for trespassing on a farm next to a nature preserve. She claimed she was testing phosphorus levels in the water."

"Save the article and search using that full name."

The living room was filled with more enthusiastic clicking, almost drowning out the background music.

"I found a Harriet Chase quoted in an article about a protest at a public meeting," Matt said.

A few minutes later, bingo!

"I found a Harriet Chase," I said. "She's the director of advocacy at the Wetlands Preservation League, Crab County Chapter. Here's her picture."

Matt leaned over and looked at my screen.

"I think we've found the right name," he said. "Now, we have to find her."

"Easier said than done."

"Hey, the internet has graced us with its bounty tonight. Oh, internet, we beg you for more."

"You're right," I said. "I'll search for her on the county property appraiser's site, in case she owns a home."

"I've got another few public-records sites that might have something."

Furious keyboard clicking ensued. The cats had stopped hissing, and Tony had stopped complaining. The only other sound was a salsa tune that somehow matched the beat of the key-clicking.

"There are no properties under her name," I said. "I guess she's a renter."

"I see a legal action associated with her name. Ah, a lawsuit initiated by her against a company: South Florida Minerals. She sued a company that sells rocks?"

My fingers raced across my keyboard.

"That's the holding company of a phosphate mining venture. From phosphates you get phosphorus, a major ingredient in fertilizers. As you know, overuse of fertilizers on farms and lawns contributes to runoff, which pollutes lakes, rivers, and, ultimately, the ocean. It causes red tide, algae blooms, fish die-offs, and the destruction of seagrass—which leaves manatees starving."

"Yep, that sounds like our girl. Can you find an address?"

"I'm going through PDFs of the legal documents now . . . Okay, here's a Jellyfish Beach address. Let's pay her a visit," I said.

"Let's hope she still lives there. And doesn't answer her door with a shotgun."

"Remember, she might be a witch. She probably doesn't need a shotgun to take us out."

"You're not filling me with confidence."

"Come on, let's go. We'll catch her off guard at this hour."

CHAPTER 20
THE TOOTHPASTE OF DEATH

"You know, surprise isn't always a good tactic for getting subjects to open up to you," Matt said as I drove through our sleeping town. "We're not the police who can intimidate them into talking."

"Someone in her group is a witch, and she's my most likely suspect. You don't want to give a witch time to prepare a spell against you."

I had volunteered to drive my car in case there were any magical pyrotechnics. It wouldn't be fair to get Matt's truck blown up. I thought it best not to mention this to him, however.

Harriet lived in a small single-story apartment complex that was old but well kept. It was within walking distance of the shops and restaurants downtown. The parking lot was brightly lit, so we waited in the car while an old man finished walking his dog and went into his apartment.

"How are we going to do this?" Matt asked. "Should I

pretend I need to talk to her about a story, or are you going to confront her right off?"

"I'm not the confrontational type. Ask her questions about the phosphate-mining lawsuit while I assess her magic. I'll take it from there."

"Okay." Matt took a gulp of air and stepped out of the car.

I led the way to apartment twelve. The lights were still on inside. I checked my watch, which said 9:45 p.m., and rang the bell. Rather late to show up at someone's door, but there was no going back now.

She opened the door the few inches allowed by the security chain and peered out.

"Yes? What do you want?"

She was younger than I had expected—around my age. Not that I was young, but I wasn't yet at the age when most crackpots and zealots become fully baked.

"Hi, I'm Matt Rosen of *The Jellyfish Beach Journal*." He flashed his ID. "Sorry for the late hour, but I wanted to ask you a quick question about your suit against South Florida Minerals."

"You're writing a story about that?" She seemed pleasantly surprised.

"Yes. It's about environmentalists fighting back against big corporations that harm our state."

"Oh, that's good to hear."

She didn't remove the security chain, which was smart. After all, we could be lying about why we were here. And, in fact, we were.

She emitted a slight scent of magic. Maybe scent was the wrong word, but it's the only way I can describe how I sensed the magic in her. It was my intuition, plus a burnt cinnamon smell and the sweet scent of lake water.

Most important, I didn't detect any black magic. An odor of sulfur was usually the big giveaway of that.

The magic coming from her was all I needed to conclude she was the witch I was seeking, and that she was not a black-magic sorceress. She appeared to be an elemental witch—probably a water witch like Tony had sensed.

I cast a quick protection spell around Matt and me, just in case we needed it.

"Is your lawsuit simply a symbolic gesture, or do you hope it will change the use of fertilizers?"

"Both," she said. "What was your name again?"

"Matt Rosen."

Her eyes narrowed. "Wait a minute, aren't you the one who emailed me about the creature—the skunk ape or whatever it was?"

Oops. Too bad Matt couldn't lie about his name, because it was on his ID.

"Yes. The munuane. I report on everything that has to do with the environment."

"I don't understand."

"Hi, I'm Missy Mindle. The creature you saw is from the wilds of Venezuela and Colombia."

"It's not a skunk ape with mutations?"

"No. Munuanes, which is what they are called, behave as protectors of the fishes and other water creatures. They are on the side of those who protect the environment."

"Then I was right—the one I saw killed those sportsmen."

"Actually, we think he's innocent, at least of those crimes."

"If so, then the police are correct and Frank Fitzwhizzle was the murderer," Harriet said.

The energy I had sensed emanating from her increased. She was brewing up some magic, hopefully simply something protective, not offensive.

"Do you think he was?" Matt asked. I knew he was probing her to see if she had planted in Frank's house whatever evidence the police had claimed to find.

"As far as I know, Frank has always used peaceful forms of protest," she replied. "And that's the point—to protest. Bringing crimes against nature to the public's attention."

"Murder brings a lot of attention," I said.

"That's true. Frank has been known to be militant in the past. He once had a ridiculous mission to liberate garden gnomes. They're not even living creatures."

I was confused. If Harriet was the murderer, she would have jumped at the chance to blame the crimes on Frank. Instead, she was being wishy-washy about it.

Then again, if she was the one who had planted evidence in Frank's home, she was doing a good job of making me doubt it. I wished she would invite us inside to talk in a more relaxed setting, but she was becoming more distrustful of us. The magical energies coming from her were growing. Too bad I couldn't use my truth spell on her. She would easily defeat it.

It was time to take the direct approach.

"Ms. Chase, you, too, are a crusader for environmental justice," I said.

She nodded.

"Especially regarding the wetlands and the creatures that inhabit them."

Another nod.

"Then you, too, had a motive to murder the fisherman and the gator hunters. What do you—"

I didn't have time to brace for the force that hit me and sent me flying from Harriet's front door. My protection spell spared me from direct bodily injury—even when I landed on the asphalt of the parking lot. But I was stunned by the impact.

A fireball shot from her open door and hit my protection bubble, disintegrating into a shower of sparks.

My spell was weakening.

I crawled behind a parked car, right before a fireball hit it. Maybe it hadn't been such a good idea to confront Harriet about the murders.

As I crouched behind the car, I couldn't see what Harriet was doing, nor how Matt was faring. When he roared like an angry beast, I figured he was on the offensive.

Something hit the roof of the car with a loud bang. The vehicle shook, and Matt tumbled from the roof to land nearby.

"Looks like the protection spell worked for you, too," I said.

"It didn't protect my pride."

Harriet's door slammed shut. I peeked around the parked car for any signs of her, but she must be barricading herself inside. Fortunately, no neighbors' lights were turning on or window blinds shifting from anyone looking outside.

"Okay," I said, trying to relax now that harm wasn't imminent. "If Harriet is the murderer, she'll come out here and kill us to keep us from implicating her. If she's innocent, she'll probably stay inside and call the police on us."

"Let's get out of here before either of those things happens."

"If she's guilty, she won't allow us to get out of here."

"No harm in trying."

Matt got up and sprinted toward my car. I had no choice but to follow.

I was in the middle of unlocking the doors when a cylinder of blackness flowed out of Harriet's front window, like ebony toothpaste squeezing out from a tube. That's the best way I could describe it. It wasn't smoke or water; the substance was pure opaque black matter, at least eight feet in diameter, that oozed toward us. It seemed to suck all the ambient light from the porch lamps into it. The black flow emanated from the spirit of death and reeked of sulfur. My protection spell wouldn't stand a chance against it.

I knew immediately that it was the product of black magic. Why was an elemental witch using black magic?

A more important question: why was I standing here like an idiot while this toothpaste of death flowed toward us?

"Matt! Run away from my car!"

"I guess this means she's guilty if she's trying to kill us."

"Run!"

We scattered. The dark matter swallowed my car, completely hiding it from view, before it turned toward me and flowed faster.

The black, toothpaste-like matter still flowed from the apartment window. It oozed across the parking lot and was now curving toward me as I retreated to the street.

I didn't know what would happen if it reached me, except that I would not survive.

I sprinted down the sidewalk, hoping Matt was running away, too. If I kept going, I should be able to escape it. The toothpaste of death couldn't follow me all the way through town, could it?

I glanced behind me, and it was gone. I stopped, panting. I should return to my car and see if it was still there and if it would start. Retreat was the only option against black magic.

The problem was, now the black goo was coming down the sidewalk at me from the opposite direction.

A food-delivery driver pulled up in front of a home that was between me and the goo and started to cross the sidewalk with a bag of food. When he saw the tubular black substance, he screamed and threw the bag of food into the home's front yard before the mass of darkness reached him. He took a photo of the tossed bag with his phone, then drove away, tires squealing. No tip for him tonight.

The toothpaste of death picked up its pace, rushing at me. While I ran away, I strengthened my protection spell. I couldn't run forever and had to stop Harriet.

The only tactic I could think of was to go to the only place she wouldn't send the flow. I would get right in her face.

I sprinted back to her apartment. The toothpaste of death now flowed from her other front window, on the opposite side of her door. I made it to the door and used an unlocking spell to open the deadbolt. Next, I used my telekinesis to slide and unlock the security chain.

Harriet was kneeling in her living room within a magic circle drawn in chalk on her wood floor. It enclosed an inverted pentagram. Black candles burned at the five points of the star, and a small copper dish near her knees held a smoldering fire that reeked of sulfur.

"Why are you using black magic?" I screamed at her.

She looked in my direction, but her eyes were all glassy.

"Elemental magic is no match for evil corporations. Time to fight evil with evil."

"Did you kill the fisherman and gator hunters? Did you murder a turtle-egg poacher and bomb the *Sea Fog*?" I asked with such authority that she answered me immediately.

"No. I would never waste my time with irrelevant little nobodies."

I didn't know a spell that would deactivate the toothpaste of death. So, I used a simpler approach. I stepped into her magic circle and erased part of the chalk-drawn circumference with my shoe, breaking her spell.

Then, I punched Harriet in the face.

She gaped at me, mouth open, eyes returning to focus. I kicked her copper bowl and stamped out the fire.

"Where did you learn black magic?" I demanded.

"None of your business."

"Someone taught you. No one can learn black magic all on their own."

"Yes, someone with much more powerful magic than your silly spell for unlocking doors." She gave a giggle that made my skin crawl, then smiled and said, "Soon, there will be more of us, and we will be unstoppable."

"Tell me who it is."

"You wouldn't know her."

"It's a woman? Do you know anything about houses of worship being defiled?"

"Get out of my house, or I'll call the police."

I turned and walked out the front door and was hit by a

force that kicked me into the parking lot. Harriet had to have the last word. Of course she did.

MY CAR WOULDN'T START. Having had the toothpaste of death flow through it, it might never start again.

Matt appeared in the parking lot. He must have been hiding nearby.

"Do you mind if we take ride shares home?" I asked him. "It doesn't seem like a good idea to call a tow truck here tonight and wait for it to show up. I'll get the car in the morning."

"Let's walk. Neither of us lives that far from here. I'll walk you to your house first."

This was one of the benefits of living in Jellyfish Beach proper. If you didn't mind living in an older home (or could afford one of the few newer ones), you could walk or ride your bike to the beach and to restaurants. It wasn't like the brand-new developments out west, such as the delayed Savanna Trace. There, you'd get a shiny new home but need to drive everywhere.

Though, you probably wouldn't have a black-magic witch living nearby driving down your property value.

It was a perfect South Florida night: warm enough to be wearing short sleeves, a pungent southeast breeze gliding in from the ocean. It was almost pleasant enough to make me forget the toothpaste of death. But not all the other death.

"I don't think Harriet is the murderer," I said.

"Really? Don't you think, by trying to kill us, she was acting like a murderer?"

"Yes, she would have killed us. She obviously has anger-management issues. But I don't think she killed those men or bombed the *Sea Fog*."

I told him about my discovery of her black magic, and that she was using it against her developer enemies.

"What's most disturbing is she mentioned someone is teaching her and others black magic. It sounded like they're forming a coven."

"Someone? Like who? You don't think. . ."

"My mother? Yes, the thought crossed my mind. It's sounding more and more like she's recovered her powers. Remember, she once sent a mosquito the size of an RV to attack me?"

"I know. It's a disturbing thought, but we have more pressing problems. Like rescuing Angela and finding the actual murderer. Or murderers."

"What if the munuanes actually are the murderers? That puts me in a real moral quandary. Expose the cryptids to the public eye or let an innocent man rot in jail. If he really is innocent, that is."

"If he's innocent, and someone did plant the evidence, then this someone knows the munuanes did it and wants to protect them."

My thoughts went to Mrs. Lupis and Mr. Lopez. Were they the type of people who would frame an innocent person? I honestly didn't know. They were too mysterious. Too weird.

But they were definitely dedicated proponents of the Friends of Cryptids Society's mission: to identify, study, and manage the cryptids of the Americas.

And quite often, manage means protect.

CHAPTER 21

PUFF PIECE

In many minds, Florida is always sunny, but not today. It rained heavily this morning. Matt and I ate breakfast beneath the awning of our usual seaside café, the wind occasionally blowing drops onto my omelet. But Matt had refused to take an inside table.

"When I eat at the beach, I want to be at the beach," he had said.

While we ate, I grew tired of small talk and brought up business. Matters were too dire now, with Angela still missing, and I didn't feel like messing around.

"Have you found anyone at the police department who will talk to you about drug running?"

"No," Matt said sheepishly. He poked at his pancakes with his fork. "I only get the generic public-relations pablum. The couple of friends I'm still in contact with there aren't involved with narcotics. The fact is, Jellyfish Beach has never had a drug problem, only small-time dealers now and then."

"What about the DEA?"

"I already told you I don't have any sources there at the moment." He slashed his pancakes with his knife.

"Then we have to talk to the chief."

"He's not going to talk to me. And what's this 'we'?"

"We're going to do a softball, human-interest interview like we did with Carrascal. The chief strikes me as a very vain man."

"With a fragile ego."

"Exactly. Reach out to his public-relations director and propose doing a puff piece to introduce him to the community. We'll let him beat his own drum for as long as he wants, but subtly slip in the questions we need to ask. If we play it right, he'll be bragging about the stuff we need to learn. Same approach we took with Carrascal."

"Carrascal has his passion—his kazoos."

"I'm sure Chief Dullart has his own passions he can't wait to talk about," I said. "His passion is most likely Chief Dullart."

"Okay. I admit it's a good idea."

"I'll bring a camera along and pretend I'm good at using it."

"Be prepared for a long wait before he can see us. In my experience, cops don't have time for puff pieces."

Matt was wrong. It turned out that the chief was eager to see us and "properly introduce himself to Jellyfish Beach."

"PLEASE BE aware that the chief cannot discuss ongoing criminal investigations," said Becka Tribeca, the public-relations director, a beautiful African American whose age suggested this was her first job.

"We would never do that," I lied. I mean, getting the chief to talk about investigations was the reason we were here. I hadn't realized he would have a media handler with him.

"So, Chief Dullart, let's start from the beginning," Matt said. "What made you decide to go into law enforcement?"

The chief leaned back in his chair, folded his hands atop his ample belly, and began in his scratchy yet high-pitched voice.

"I believed I had a calling to protect the good and the vulnerable and to take the thugs who prey upon them off the streets. I believe in justice and accountability. And I have always had the courage of my convictions. Law enforcement seemed like the natural career path for me. Plus, my uncle, Bobby, was a cop."

I was already getting bored. While the chief spoke, I took a few pictures of him, then pretended to study them on my camera's rear screen.

"You moved to Jellyfish Beach from Pigsknuckle, Arkansas. Is that where you grew up?" Matt asked.

"Yes. And I began my policing career at the Pigsknuckle P.D. I rose to captain in only twenty years, the fastest rise in the department's history."

"How many officers are on staff there?"

"Um, three. You got a problem with that?"

"Of course not. What made you want to move to Florida, of all places?"

"The opportunity at the Jellyfish Beach Police Department seemed perfect for me. I knew I could transform this organization into one of the best in the state. And my wife really wanted to live near the beach. She couldn't wait to get out of Pigsknuckle."

"Does your wife have a career?"

"Let's not talk about my wife, okay?"

He's the one who mentioned her, I thought. I saw his jowls going red, like during that press conference.

Matt flipped the page of his notebook. He didn't appear to be writing very much.

"How do you enjoy living in Florida?" he asked.

"I love the outdoors. In Arkansas, I was a member of the Pigsknuckle Bassmasters and won a few tournaments. I also was a big duck hunter. Here in Florida, you've got all that, plus the many saltwater fishing opportunities. I just love it."

The chief seemed in better spirits now. His jowls had faded back to a normal flesh tone.

"Are you a member of any local clubs?"

"Yep. The Crab County Sportsmen's Club and the Police Benevolent Association. Can we talk about how transformational my leadership is?"

"Sure. Let's approach it this way: what's your assessment of the police department here—its strengths and weaknesses? What changes would you like to make?"

"This is fundamentally a solid police force. Good, well-trained people. We could use more resources, and I'll work with the city commission to bring about that. What this department lacked was leadership. Unfortunately, I had to fire the officer who served as interim chief because of incompetence. Now that I'm here, I'm demonstrating what strong, smart leadership can accomplish."

"Yeah, I meant to ask you about the interim chief, Elaine Vasquez. Word on the street was that you two didn't get along.

Did she resent you because she expected to be appointed chief after Chief McNeil retired?"

Matt was more animated now. He was sniffing out an actual story, instead of just being a stenographer for a puff piece. But we were here for a puff piece.

"I don't care about her emotions," the chief said, his jowls turning red again. "She was incompetent, and the entire department suffered for it."

"I heard you screamed at her for not respecting you enough."

"We cannot comment on personnel issues," said his handler, Becka Tribeca.

"Sorry," Matt said. He saw me glaring at him and realized he had gone off the script. "Chief, I've also heard that morale here is outstanding ever since you came on board."

The jowls lightened by two shades. Then they jiggled as the chief nodded with enthusiasm.

"Every officer and staff member knows their roles and goals now. They know they'll be held accountable for their performance and be rewarded when it's good."

"Awesome," Matt said, appearing bored again. "What are the challenges the department faces in terms of crime?"

"Jellyfish Beach is blessed with a low crime rate. But there are offenses we will crack down on. Parking laws will be more strictly enforced. Scofflaws who don't pick up their dogs' poop will be fined. Senior-on-senior violence at bingo nights must end."

"I didn't realize that was a thing."

"Oh, yes. Lots of aggression at these events. Fortunately, there have been no serious injuries."

"What about drug crimes?" Matt asked, staring intently at the chief.

"Almost non-existent. We'll continue to be vigilant."

"Is there any smuggling going on via boats?"

The chief's eyes narrowed slightly, and his jowls darkened again.

"That would be under the purview of the Coast Guard and the DEA."

"But do you know of any locals who are suspected of drug smuggling?"

"We don't have any active cases involving smuggling," the chief said through clenched jaws.

"We can't discuss specific investigations," Tribeca said.

"I believe the DEA has an active case or two in the area," Matt muttered.

"What was that? You were mumbling."

"I said the DEA is investigating smugglers here, sir. Drugs from outside the US. Transferred to smaller boats that come in through the inlet."

"We will fully cooperate if the feds need our assistance."

"I just figured that as the local law-enforcement agency, you would know about this activity."

"We can't comment," Tribeca said.

"Of course, my apologies. The only reason I bring up this subject is to hypothesize that the recent string of murders could be about smugglers killing witnesses."

BAM! The chief pounded his desk with his fist. I jumped and almost dropped the camera.

"We have a suspect in custody for the murders, and

evidence that proves the deceased were victims of eco-terrorism."

"We can't comment on ongoing investigations," Tribeca futilely said.

The chief's jowls and much of his face were reaching dangerous shades of purple. My nurse's instincts put me on alert for a cardiac event.

"Are these incidents of eco-terrorism limited to only Jellyfish Beach?" Matt asked softly.

"We can't comment—"

"Shut up, Becka," the chief ordered. "I'll tell you this: the suspect is a lone-wolf killer and has only operated here, because this is where he lives. When the case goes to trial, you'll learn all about it. Until then, don't ask me about it."

"I believe we're done here," Becka said.

"Do you have a message you'd like to send to the local community?" Matt asked with a big, fake smile.

"The citizens of Jellyfish Beach can rest assured that the safety of their families and their property is in the best hands."

"Perfect, Chief," Matt said. "Great quote to end the article. Thank you for your time."

The chief nodded, fanning his red, sweaty face with a file folder as Tribeca escorted us out.

"You simply can't resist pushing too far," I said to Matt as we walked to my car in the parking lot behind the station.

"I can't resist being me. Now, why is he being so opaque about the drug smuggling? He would brag about his fight against the smugglers if he wanted to, no matter what his PR flack says."

I had a dark thought. I hated to say it, but I said it anyway.

"Do you think he's on Carrascal's payroll to look the other way?"

"That's exactly what I think."

THE MEMORY POTION filled a quart-sized glass bottle. I handed it to Philip and Dorita at their condo, along with the photos and wedding ring I had borrowed.

"This was the largest batch I could make without it losing strength," I said.

"Does it have a 'use-by' date?" Philip asked with a smile.

"No, and it doesn't need to be refrigerated. But keep the lid screwed on tight. I figured this should last you for a long while. The dosage is one tablespoon per day, and I don't recommend taking it daily. Save it for the days when you truly don't feel like yourself, Dorita. When you run out, I'll make another batch."

"Will you accept payment for all your trouble?" Philip asked.

"The only payment I want is to see happiness on your faces."

When I bumped into them later, the happiness radiated from them like they were a pair of lighthouses.

"You're a genius, Missy," Philip said.

Dorita took my hands and stared into my eyes. At first, I was afraid she was going to mesmerize me. Instead, she kissed me on the cheek.

"I'll never be able to thank you enough, Missy."

It made me miss being a full-time nurse. And feel immensely satisfied that I was becoming a powerful witch, despite the supposed dangers that came with power.

What could be wrong with developing the power to help others?

CHAPTER 22

CRAB COUNTY SPORTSMEN'S CLUB

After having researched environmental groups, I decided to do the same with the Crab County Sportsmen's Club. I hoped to find someone Matt and I could speak to about Chief Dullart. It wasn't likely that a fellow fishing enthusiast would know if the chief had an association with Carrascal, but the club member might notice if the chief seemed flush with cash.

When I found the club's website and went to its About Us page, my eyes popped open. I grabbed my phone.

"Matt, I was looking up the Crab County Sportsmen's Club, and you'll never guess who the president is."

"You're right. I'll never guess."

"Bill Tendrix, the captain of the *Sea Fog*. We should ask him if he has any knowledge of the chief suddenly becoming a big spender."

"Would Tendrix know that?"

"It's worth a try. Meet me at the marina. The *Sea Fog* will dock soon after its afternoon trip."

Captain Tendrix was not happy to see us. After the last passenger had disembarked, we cornered him in his office on the dock.

"Now what?" he asked.

"We wanted to ask you about Chief Dullart," I said. "He told us he's a member of the Crab County Sportsmen's Club, and I see that you're the president."

"He *was* a member."

"He quit?"

"No, we kicked him out."

"Why?"

"I'd rather not say. I don't want us to be sued for defamation. Let's just say he didn't get along with the other members."

"How did he react to being expelled?"

"I'd rather not say."

"It's interesting that someone tried to blow you up with a pipe bomb," Matt said.

"Come on, no one's going to try to kill someone over getting kicked out of a club."

"Then, you agree it's more likely that a drug runner did it?"

Tendrix sighed and rubbed his eyes. "When you're out on the water every single day, you sometimes see strange things happening on other boats. You know, topless sunbathing, migrants packed aboard, movies being shot. Sometimes, you see two boats tied together, and they're transferring fish they caught to get around the bag limits. There might have been once or twice I saw stuff being transferred between boats that wasn't fish."

"Drugs?" I asked.

He shrugged. "Packages. Who knows what was inside?"

"They would do that in broad daylight?"

"Yeah. They don't stand out when there are lots of boats on the water. At night, surveillance flights take a closer look at what the boats are doing out there."

"Did you recognize the boats?" Matt asked.

Tendrix shook his head. He seemed evasive to me.

"The *Sea Fog* is unmistakable," Matt said. "If you passed boats doing something illegal, and they suspected you knew what they were doing, they would know exactly where to find you."

"Yeah." He glanced out the window at Rivas's empty slip.

"Sorry. There's nothing else I can tell you, and I have a lot of paperwork to finish."

We took the hint. Before I left the tiny office, I asked Tendrix if he had a list of the Sportsmen's Club's membership.

"Why?"

"It would be very helpful and would mean we wouldn't have to visit you again and again."

He muttered something you wouldn't want a child to hear and opened a drawer. He handed me three pages stapled together with names printed on both sides.

"Thank you," I said.

Matt stood by Rivas's slip, staring out at the channel. I followed his gaze and saw Rivas turning from the Intracoastal into the channel leading to the marina.

The commercial fisherman's twenty-six-foot center-console boat chugged slowly toward us through the maze of finger piers. He made quick, subtle adjustments of the wheel and throttle. When he saw us, his face darkened.

As he pulled into his slip, he threw Matt the bowline in a challenging manner. Matt caught it and tied it to a cleat.

"You guys have too much time on your hands," Rivas said, cutting off his outboard engine and jumping onto the dock to tie the other lines.

"No, we're just very fond of you," I said.

I studied Rivas's boat carefully. He had four fishing rods jutting up from their holders, which gave the impression he'd been fishing today, but the boat looked too clean compared to the first time we had met him, when he had returned with a cooler full of fish. That time, he had hosed the fish slime and scales from his deck after we had spoken to him.

"How was the fishing today?" I asked.

"Good." He tried to ignore me as he secured the boat.

"What did you catch?"

He glared at me. "Wahoo. Cobia."

"That's awesome," I said. "Can I see them?"

"No. What do you guys want?"

"We just had a couple of questions," Matt said as he leaned against a dock piling, acting relaxed.

I did the same, hoping our relaxed airs would put Rivas at ease. What I was actually doing was concentrating on casting a spell that would allow me to see inside the large built-in cooler in the boat's stern.

"We had some questions about munuanes," Matt said. "Almost nobody else knows about them."

"I've told you everything I know."

"Not really. You didn't tell us you were helping them."

Rivas froze. "What the heck are you talking about?"

"You helped them find empty homes to live in."

"They live in the wilderness. You saw one living on Beer Can Island."

"It was living there temporarily. Until you found much better accommodations in an oceanfront mansion for the patriarch and his family."

"You're crazy. Why are you making this stuff up?"

"We saw them in the mansion," I said. I shouldn't have spoken because it interfered with my spell-casting.

"The mansion belongs to Felix Carrascal," Matt said. "After that, we found the munuane family living in another home owned by Carrascal."

"Never heard of him."

"He grew up in a village in Colombia. You grew up in Venezuela. He knows about munuanes, too."

"I don't know him. Just because we grew up in the same region of the world doesn't mean we'd know each other. We're from different countries."

"Countries where the munuanes are from."

"So what? Why would I help munuanes?"

"That's what we want to know," Matt said. "Is it because Carrascal asked you to? Is he sentimental about the creatures?"

"I told you I don't know the man. Now, get out of here before I have you arrested for trespassing."

"Do you work for Carrascal?"

Rivas was beyond angry. He had stepped off the boat and now put his face into Matt's.

"Get out of here before I blow your head off." He pulled up his shirt to reveal a handgun in a holster.

"Okay," Matt said, his relaxed air completely gone. "Step away from me, and we'll leave now."

Rivas stepped aside, and Matt began to retreat down the dock, but stopped to wait for me. Rivas looked at me, too.

I remained leaning against the piling, finishing my penetration spell. The Latin words I recited were too low for anyone else to hear.

"What's wrong with her?" Rivas asked. "She's talking to herself."

The energy flowed from me and through the walls of the cooler on Rivas's boat. Energy flowed back the other way into my head, where an image formed.

An image of the empty interior of the cooler. No fish were inside. Whatever Rivas had been up to, it didn't involve fishing.

Any guesses? You think he might have been transporting some products?

I did.

BETWEEN MUNUANES, murderers, and black-magic maniacs, it wasn't safe for me to sleep without placing wards around my house. I was shocked the next morning when I stepped out my front door to get the daily newspaper from my driveway. The wards had been defeated overnight.

This was confirmed when I saw the machete, its blade stuck in my garage door. It impaled a paper note against the wood.

No drug runner did this. It had been a magician of some sort, one experienced enough to defeat the wards.

I can find other imps, the note said. *But you have only one iguana familiar. Stop interfering with my magic or your lizard will end up as iguana stew.*

It was signed Ophelia Lawthorne. My mother.

Obviously, Jellyfish Beach had not escaped her menace. It looked more and more inevitable that I would engage in personal combat with her. I didn't know if I had the strength and power to prevail.

Tony came around the side of the house and read the note.

"Does this mean you'll let me smoke indoors now?"

CHAPTER 23
SOMETHING IN COMMON

"No. The reason it matters that his cooler was empty is because he told us he was out fishing all day," Matt said over the phone to Special Agent Janscomb of the DEA. "No, he didn't have 'bad luck.' He's a commercial fisherman. They almost always come back with fish. And if he had a bad day, why lie about it?"

Matt sighed and rolled his eyes at me as I drove him home.

"Do you consider him a suspect in the drug smuggling?" he asked Janscomb. "Of course, I know you can't officially comment on that, but you can grunt in affirmation. No? You can't give me a simple grunt? I told you Rivas has a connection with Felix Carrascal . . . Yes, that matters! Come on, I promised you this is off the record. All I ask is for some sort of noncommittal confirmation that I'm barking up the right tree."

Matt cursed and stuck his phone in his pocket.

"Janscomb won't give me anything."

"Don't whine," I said. "It's not a good image for you."

"He could have thrown us a bone and admitted Rivas is a suspect."

"You and I both know he's running drugs for Carrascal. He's also probably responsible for putting the munuanes in the homes. We don't know if he's doing it with Carrascal's permission, but I wouldn't be surprised, since Carrascal spoke so fondly of the creatures. In fact, it might be his idea to put them there."

"Just because he's fond of a childhood legend?"

"It could be personal. Maybe he's interacted with them before."

"How could anyone be fond of ogres?" Matt rubbed the back of his head. "One of them bonked me in the noggin just because I didn't release a fish soon enough."

"You weren't going to release it at all. Don't rewrite history. And all the munuane did was hit you on the head. He didn't kill you. Assuming your assailant was a munuane."

"I told you I smelled a funky monster smell."

"There's more than one monster out there in the world."

"And you're trying to find all of them, thanks to your buddies in the Friends of Cryptids Society."

I laughed. It hadn't fully sunk in that my future career path would involve constant encounters with different monsters in the name of science. Well, I guess someone's got to do it.

I pulled up in front of Matt's bungalow.

"Speaking of fish, I have some freshly caught snapper," Matt said. "How about I cook you dinner?"

"Sure. As long as the fish are legal."

Matt laughed. "They most definitely are."

Matt popped open a beer and poured me a glass of wine.

While he dredged the fish filets in flour and panko, I sat in his breakfast nook and looked at the membership list of the Crab County Sportsmen's Club. Almost three quarters of the names were men. I recognized some of them as prominent local business leaders, such as attorneys, doctors, car dealers, and the like. None were customers at the botanica, no surprise.

A few names were familiar, but I couldn't place them.

"Does the name Gerald Holstein ring a bell with you?"

"If I remember correctly, that is the fisherman who was murdered at the boat ramp." Matt dropped the filets into a pan of sizzling olive oil. "It makes sense he would be a member of the club."

"What about Richard Alfini?"

"Sounds familiar."

"Bobby Ray Higgles?"

"Him, too."

I pulled out my phone and started searching, filtering for news articles.

"They're the gator hunters who were murdered," I said.

Matt turned from the stove with a surprised look. "Well, again, they're sportsmen. I guess everyone who's anyone in the hunting and fishing world joins this club."

He was most likely correct, but I was getting the feeling this was more than a coincidence.

I don't know if Matt was hoping it would be a romantic meal, but as we ate the fish, rice, and green beans, I continued studying the membership list and searching for names that looked at all familiar.

I found a connection that made me gasp.

"Thong Man was a member, too."

"Who?"

"Max Massey. The man who ruined the press conference on the beach by doing exercises in his thong bathing suit. He's the one who was murdered while allegedly stealing sea turtle eggs."

"Wow. I thought he was just some crazy old snowbird."

"He's a former orthodontist and member in good standing at the club. All the victims were members, except for the tourist killed in the blast on the Sea Fog. But the bomb was meant for Captain Tendrix, the president of the club."

"Does every fisherman and hunter in Crab County belong to this club? A few of my friends do. I guess I'm the only sportsman who doesn't."

"You can apply online, if you want."

"This club is not good for your health. Still, the victims being on the list is all a big coincidence, right? You don't think the munuanes got ahold of the list, do you?"

"No, I don't. I seriously doubt they're that smart. Maybe we should rethink everything about these crimes. We've always assumed the victims were killed because of something they were doing when they were killed. Like violating nature. Which is why we assumed the munuanes did it."

"Or witnessing drug-smuggling activity. I really believe that's the best theory."

"Maybe there's something else the victims have in common."

"Just being in the club? There's no way someone is going to kill everyone on the membership list. That's too much work, even for the most ambitious serial killer."

I shook my head. "I don't know. There's got to be something."

"I'm putting money on the drug-smuggling theory. Drug traffickers kill witnesses all the time."

"Yeah." But I couldn't let it rest.

After I returned home, I fed the kitties and a complaining iguana. While I sipped a cup of tea, I thought about the murders.

There was one loose thread that needed tugging.

ELAINE VASQUEZ, former interim chief of the Jellyfish Beach Police Department, graciously agreed to a video meeting with Matt and me the next day. I say graciously, but it was clear she held a grudge against the man who had fired her.

"I don't feel any resentment," she said, clearly lying. "I believe Chief Dullart is an idiot and a psycho, that's all."

Vasquez had quickly found a high-ranking position at a police department in North Florida, which was why we held a video call instead of visiting her. Matt and I signed on from our homes.

"I heard everyone believed you would be appointed chief of police after Chief McNeil retired," Matt said. "You had the most seniority. I was surprised they hired Dullart."

"Me, too," she said with a bitter smile. She was in her forties and looked smart and tough. "The rank-and-file officers were all behind me, but the city commission wanted someone with more experience. What they really wanted was an older white guy. I thought I would move back to my previous position, but Dullart had a problem with me from day one."

"Clashing personalities?" I asked.

"Clashing everything. Dullart is a big bully who's secretly insecure. He saw me as a threat because I was doing his job really well and everyone respected me. He had a major issue with being shown proper respect."

"How so?" Matt asked.

"He expected all personnel to treat him like a military officer. Standing at attention, throwing around lots of 'sir, yes, sir!' That kind of thing. In his first few weeks, he wrote up half a dozen people. And there aren't many people on the force in Jellyfish Beach. As for me, he liked to belittle me in front of others. Make fun of my accent. Disagree with everything I said. It was humiliating."

"That guy is a real piece of work," I said.

"He's the biggest jerk I've ever come across," Vasquez said with a bitter smile. "I have to admit, I enjoyed watching his recent press conferences. He looked like such a fool. And he couldn't control his temper when he was interrupted by all that crazy stuff. That is exactly what he dreads the most—people making a mockery of him."

"Do you know why he was kicked out of the Crab County Sportsmen's Club?" I asked.

"No, though I'm sure he was a jerk to everyone."

"Do you think he ever got violent with people who mocked him?"

"Yes, I do. I'm ashamed to admit it, but I tried to find out dirt about him through a friend who knows someone in Arkansas law enforcement. There's a rumor going around that

Dullart's wife prefers having an open marriage. Dullart prefers they didn't. So, the gossip was that she was having some flings behind his back, and he really flipped out when he found out about them. He allegedly assaulted some guys."

"His wife's lovers?"

"Yeah. And men who made fun of him for being a cuckold."

"He didn't get fired for that?"

"No. The guys he beat up weren't in law enforcement, and since he was a high-ranking cop in a small town, his victims were too afraid to speak out against him. I'm sure Dullart saw the writing on the wall and knew he wouldn't last much longer in Pigsknuckle. That's why he applied for the job here. And I think his wife wanted to move to Florida."

"I can't believe our city commission didn't do a better job at vetting him," Matt said.

"You know how it is—the old boy's network gives the old white guy a pass."

"Do you think he's capable of doing more than beating up someone he's angry at?"

"I can't speculate on something like that. I've already said more than I should have, and only because of your promise of this conversation being off the record."

"Yes, and I keep my word," Matt said.

"All I can say is watch out for him," Vasquez said. "He's like a powder keg that could blow up at any moment. And you be careful. Don't push him, or you'll regret it."

We thanked her and ended the video call. Matt and I stayed on so we could discuss the interview together.

"We have to look into this," I said. "I want to know if his

wife is pursuing an open marriage here in Jellyfish Beach. I guess asking her is out of the question."

"Absolutely out of the question."

"I could use my truth-telling spell on her."

"No. If Chief Dullart finds out we've spoken to her, he'll come after us."

"We also need to speak with members of the Sportsmen's Club and find out why they're dropping like flies."

"You think his wife was involved with one of them?"

"Could be. Or there was something else that made those men mock Dullart."

"That's your theory now? These men were murdered by the chief because they mocked him? Sounds like a real stretch to me."

"I read somewhere the most common motives for murder are money, love, and honor."

Matt was silent for a while, then nodded.

"For humans," he said. "I don't know what motives munuanes have."

"I thought we gave up going down that road."

"This new road scares me. The chief scares me more than drug runners and ogres."

He laughed, but it was nervous laughter.

"I had a thought," I said. "Can you find out if there are any unsolved murders in and around Pigsknuckle, Arkansas? You know, with victims that match the profile of the ones here."

"Are you serious?"

"I am."

"I'll look into it." He signed off from the meeting, and I was left staring at myself on the screen, sitting there all alone.

But that's me, right? Missy, all alone. No one sharing my home except for two felines, a reptile, and a ghost. And it's because of my choosing. After my husband left me for someone else, and soon afterward was murdered, there was nothing stopping me from finding someone else to love.

The only thing stopping me was me.

As to why, I told myself the easy explanation. I wanted to avoid the heartbreak of another failed relationship. I needed time to be strong in myself without needing someone to lean on.

The easy explanation seemed a little too easy.

My second, slightly more complicated, excuse was that my career had been too demanding to provide time for finding a suitable partner. Well, my career nearly broke me, so I quit my job as an intensive-care nurse and went into home-health nursing.

Normally, a career move like that would mean less money, but significantly less stress.

But leave it to me to choose a job where I cared for vampires and werewolves. In case it wasn't obvious, dealing with monsters is decidedly *not* less stressful.

Another, more recent, explanation for my remaining single was my growth as a witch. There are many witches who celebrate their craft as a form of feminism. That's not what I'm talking about.

I'm talking about growing more powerful and effective. This requires dedication and concentration. The demands and mind-games of a romantic partner would only be a distraction.

Just so you know, I'm not a megalomaniac. I'm not saying I'm destined for greatness and can't afford to have some guy holding me back. I'm talking about the need for asceticism, monasticism, being married to the magic and the spiritual world.

I know it sounds weird, but if you were a witch with growing power, you'd understand.

The video app was still open, and I was staring at my image on the computer screen. It was a little creepy.

And I realized all this talk of Dullart and his wife had truly disgusted me. The thought of a romantic partner wanting an open relationship was sad. A partner turning all possessive and psychotic was scary.

Right now, I simply had no desire for a romantic relationship, even with a sweet, laid-back guy like Matt.

MATT DIDN'T CALL me back until the next day.

"I searched a lot of news archives," he said. "Then, I spoke with the Pigsknuckle Police Department and a local reporter. You realize that anywhere people live, there are always unsolved disappearances and murder cases."

"Yes. Get on with it."

"Two local businessmen in Pigsknuckle died while fishing. It was meant to look like drownings, but there is evidence they were strangled before they went into the water."

"Any connection between them and Chief Dullart?"

"The only connection I could find was that both men were members of the Pigsknuckle Bassmasters Club, which our friend also belonged to. I could try to speak with other members of the club."

"No. That would take too much time. We need to speak to members of the Sportsmen's Club here. There are more than a hundred of them, and it might take a while before we find one who knows anything."

"Let me start with a couple of buddies of mine who are members. It's much better than cold calling. Just be aware that if anyone suspected the chief, word would have come out by now."

"Of course. But no one would suspect that he's a psycho."

While Matt made his inquiries, I had unfinished business to attend to.

CHAPTER 24
REUNIONS

I found Mrs. Lupis's number in my phone's history and called it.

"Thank you for calling The Friends of Cryptids Society of the Americas," her voicemail said in a robotic voice. "Mrs. Lupis, Co-Director of Ambiguous Activities, is unable to take your call. Please leave a message."

This was the first time I had heard her actual title. It was as weird as she was.

"Mrs. Lupis, this is Missy Mindle. Please call me so we can discuss—"

My doorbell rang. I knew who it was, so I disconnected the call.

"Fancy meeting you here," I said as I opened the door for Mrs. Lupis and Mr. Lopez.

"You wanted to speak with me about rescuing Angela?"

"Well, yes." Why bother asking her how she knew? "I saved munuane fur from the townhome they were staying in

—fur flecked with gray, so I'm assuming it belonged to the patriarch. I can use the fur with my spell to find him, like I did before, but I don't think another raid would be a good idea."

"Because he'd be expecting it?" Mrs. Lupis asked.

"And might harm his hostage?" Mr. Lopez added.

"Yes, exactly. Mr. Lopez, you said we couldn't expect the munuane to exchange Angela for his family in good faith. I disagree. I believe if we want him to behave in our world, we must behave honorably ourselves and return his family to him."

He nodded. "We have arrived at the same conclusion. Contrary to the depictions of munuanes in the legends as slow-witted, savage killers of humans, our linguists and other experts have found that they are gentle and intelligent."

"Intelligent might be an overstatement," Mrs. Lupis said.

"Intelligent enough to be reasoned with. We have finished all the data gathering we can ethically accomplish with moderately intelligent creatures held against their will. And we are prepared to release them."

"To the patriarch in exchange for Angela, of course," Mrs. Lupis added.

"How do you propose we contact the patriarch?"

"The family conveyed to us where he most likely is hiding, but we couldn't find him."

"You've already been looking for him?" I asked.

They both nodded.

"I see. You're here to see me because you believe magic is the only way to find him."

They nodded.

"And because you reached out to me," Mrs. Lupis said. "It was as if today was destined to happen."

"Except this time, we need you to try a different spell," Mr. Lopez said. "The mother munuane—whose fur you found in the mansion and used last time—said she had sensed something magical was going on when you searched with it. Now, her mate will know what you're up to if your spell uses his energy to locate him. Similarly, he might sense the magical activity if you use the same spell to find Angela instead."

"A spell that merely sends a message to him about a meeting spot would be sufficient," said Mr. Lopez.

"No," Mrs. Lupis said. "Send the message to Angela. Missy would need a linguist with her to communicate with the munuane. Angela can convey the message to him with the magic she uses to communicate with non-humans."

"I will need to devise a new spell to find her," I said.

"Angela could accomplish this task, but, well, you know."

And I had been hoping to advance my magical abilities under her tutelage. But, well, you know.

I had other mentors of sorts, the ghost of a former accomplished wizard and an iguana. Tony was off somewhere, probably destroying neighbors' gardens, not answering my telepathic calls.

To summon Don Mateo, all I had to do was open my lingerie drawer and call for him.

And call again, and again, until my voice got hoarse.

He finally appeared, transparent at first and then fully opaque. Wearing his seventeenth-century waistcoat and breeches, he bent over my dresser, examining the lacy red panties I haven't worn since I was married.

"Don Mateo! Good to see you. How has the Other Side been treating you since we saw each other last?"

"It's been quite boring as usual," he said in his archaic Spanish accent after giving me a courtly bow. "It's nice to take a little outing to the material world. How may I be of service to you?"

"I don't have telepathic abilities other than with Tony, and I need to send a message to someone whose location is unknown to me."

"Ah. I have learned of a magical device, not much bigger than a snuff box or playing cards, that gives you the power of writing a message to someone or even speaking to them instantly, no matter how far away they are."

"Yes, they're called cellphones. They're not magical, and the person I need to reach does not have hers with her."

"Oh. Just when I thought I was understanding this world you inhabit."

"No worries. The magic you used in your era is just as effective today."

"Tell me about this person you wish to reach. Is she a normal human?"

"She's a mage."

"Ah. What school of magedom does she follow?"

"I don't know. There are different schools?"

"If you don't know, you weren't meant to know. We can reach her, nevertheless. There are certain principles of magic that are universal. The first of which is the power of one's name. This holds true for many systems of magic and in many cultures throughout human history."

"Her name is Angela Davie."

"Are you certain that's her true name? This won't work if she's using an alias or stage name."

"No, I'm not absolutely certain. Sorry."

"Well then, I suppose we shall see if it is by whether the spell works. Now, allow me to calculate how to convert it into the elemental magic you use. Prepare your quaint little magic circle now."

"It's not quaint. It actually works."

Don Mateo, regardless of how powerful a wizard he once was, could not cast the spell. He was just a ghost, after all. He would have to be my coach while I did it.

I quickly drew a circle large enough to contain myself on my tile floor with a dry-erase marker. It was a close-to-perfect circle, since I'd had a lot of practice at this.

"Now, gather your energies, and repeat my words, touching the points of the pentagram corresponding to each element we address."

I didn't need to draw a pentagram within the circle. Visualizing it worked just as well.

"The element of Earth, you represent truth and the physicality of the true name of Angela Davie. I beseech you to find her."

I repeated these words while touching the lower-left point of the pentagram.

"Water, you represent the flesh of the person whose true name is Angela Davie. I beseech you to find her."

I repeated Don Mateo's words while touching the upper-right point.

We moved on to Wind, which represented the words of Angela's parents when they named her and every subsequent person who has called her name. Then came Fire, which symbolized the passion evoked by one's name. Finally, came Spirit, which literally connected with the spirit of the person via her true name.

"Angela Davie, through your true name, I find you, and I speak now to you," I repeated.

Suddenly, an image of her face came into my mind. She was in a mangrove forest. Her location didn't matter; only that she could hear me.

"Angela, can you hear me?"

She smiled and nodded.

"We want to return the munuane's family to him if he frees you in return. We will meet you tonight, just after sunset, at Egret Park."

She nodded and mouthed some words. Seconds later, they came into my brain.

"Thank you. We will be there. Please let this not be a trap."

"Assure him we do this in good faith."

The image of her face slowly faded away, leaving a view of my kitchen floor with Don Mateo hovering just outside of the circle.

"Good job, young lady. You do have power and potential in you."

"I'm not young."

"You are a mere infant compared to me," said the ghost before disappearing.

I RODE with the munuanes in the back of a passenger van driven by Mr. Lopez. No need to cart the ogres around in a moving van like before. Tonight, they were awake and cooperative, eager to be reunited with their patriarch.

I was not enjoying the funky, musky odor of my fellow passengers. Mrs. Lupis had assured me the family had recently bathed, and you'd think that since they'd spent several days not living in a swamp, they wouldn't offend my nose. But I don't judge. Monsters will be monsters. You have to let them be themselves.

The family communicated with their grunts and squeaks while I looked out the window nervously, hoping no one would spot the strange creatures in the van despite the falling darkness. It didn't help that the munuanes sat with one foot on the seat so a knee would be high enough for its eye to look out the window.

Sure enough, while we sat at a red light, I glanced outside to see a boy staring at us from the back seat of a car. He stuck his finger in his nose, and the youngest munuane did the same. The boy and the munuane both erupted in giggles as the light turned green. I wonder what the boy said to his parents.

Egret Park was located on the Intracoastal, opposite the mangrove forest that abutted the townhome community where the munuanes had been living. The park was closed for the day, but Mr. Lopez fished a key from his pocket and opened the padlock. Why he had the key would be a question for another day.

Mr. Lopez drove along a windy road through mangrove and sea-grape trees until we reached a parking area near the water. There was a narrow beach, suitable for launching kayaks and paddle boards. As we piled out of the van, Angela and the senior munuane came into view on the beach, silhouetted against water that shimmered in the moonlight.

The munuane family ran excitedly toward their patriarch. Perhaps run is the wrong word. It was more of a loping, just like when they had chased me at the oceanfront mansion. When you have your eyes on your knees, running like a human would make you dizzy.

As the family reunited, I witnessed another munuane oddity. Instead of hugging like I expected, they smacked each other affectionately on the head. Without eyes there, each head was a mouth, a nose, and a huge skull covered in fur. Getting smacked wouldn't bother them a bit, though it seemed odd to me. Again, monsters will be monsters.

Angela and I, however, hugged. Then she looked at Mrs. Lupis and Mr. Lopez. Her expression said she wanted to hug them, but theirs said, "Don't you dare."

"We're glad you're free," they both said.

"The munuanes told me . . ." Angela trailed off as she glanced behind her.

The munuane family had slipped away.

"They told me they didn't kill any humans," she continued. "But the father did admit to attacking some humans in a non-lethal manner, including a man on a personal watercraft and a fisherman who was going to keep a snook illegally."

"That would be my friend, Matt," I said. "Did the father know who killed the humans?"

"No, he didn't. He knew nothing about the murders. He told me something interesting about the homes, though. A boat captain discovered the family's lair and offered to bring them all to a safe place to live—the mansion. After Missy and her crew discovered us there, the captain took us all by boat to the smaller place."

"Did the boat captain have a scar on his cheek?" I asked.

"He did."

"It was Raul Rivas. That means he took part in a kidnapping. I'll let the police know."

"Don't," Mrs. Lupis said. "That would lead to the authorities finding out about the munuanes."

"I agree," Angela said.

I shrugged. "Suit yourself. I was only hoping to get a drug smuggler locked up."

"Angela," Mrs. Lupis said, "we're sympathetic to all you've been through, but we would like to meet with you as soon as possible for a debriefing."

"Thank you," Angela replied. "I wasn't mistreated and never feared for my life. I'll get over it, as long as I don't have to eat fish for every meal again. We can have the meeting tomorrow."

"We learned from the munuanes that they know of dozens of their species that have migrated to Florida," Mr. Lopez said. "We'll need to get a better idea of their total population."

"Oh, my," I said. "It's true: *everyone* is moving to Florida."

CHAPTER 25
DESPERATE MEASURES

"I tell ya, it wasn't me," insisted Tony. I had caught him crawling into the garage through the open side window.

"My neighbor says she saw an iguana that matches your size swimming in her pool and using it as a toilet."

"Iguanas do that when we swim. We can't help it. But why would you assume it was me when South Florida is filled with iguanas?"

"Because I haven't seen any at all in our neighborhood in a long time."

"Thanks to the lawn-maintenance guys. They come after us with machetes, the savages."

"Please don't swim in her pool anymore. Go to the canal across the street if you have an irrepressible urge to swim."

"I tell ya, it wasn't me."

"Why do you smell like chlorine?"

"Um, let me get back to you on that."

The doorbell rang, sparing Tony from more questioning. I went inside to find Matt at the front door. He looked haunted.

"What's wrong, Matt?"

"I talked to a few of my buddies who belong to the Sportsmen's Club. It's looking to me like there's something to our theory about the chief."

"Come inside, and sit down," I said.

When we were seated in the kitchen, Matt continued his story.

"There are rumors that the chief's wife slept with someone in the club. It's like a running joke that guys share behind the chief's back to show they're in on the gossip. My friends aren't in the inner circle, so they couldn't give me any specifics, except for one story."

"Go on."

"You realize I haven't exactly been respectful to the chief. I put jokes in my questions when the guy with the thong bathing suit made a mockery of that press conference."

"Before he ended up dead."

"You see why I'm nervous? That man didn't fit the profile of someone who would steal turtle eggs to make some extra money. He was a successful orthodontist who retired after a minor brush with the law."

"And he had an unfortunate sense of humor. Now, tell me the story you heard."

"Okay. So, at the club's annual holiday banquet, there was some incident in which the chief's wife tossed a glass of wine in the president's face."

"Captain Tendrix?"

"Yeah. Most people assumed he had offended her, but no

one could say exactly what he did. One of my friends said he heard they had slept together, and Tendrix dumped her. And you know what happened to the *Sea Fog*. My guess is that the other guys who were murdered were too careless in their mockery of the chief."

"Why hasn't anyone come forward with this?"

"They didn't make the connection between the murders."

"We must talk to Tendrix right away."

"Boy, is that going to be awkward!"

"Too bad," I said. "We have to do it. You're a thick-skinned journalist, after all."

"My skin is not thick enough to stop a bullet."

THIS TIME, Captain Tendrix didn't even try to hide his displeasure at seeing us.

"I don't have time to be dragged down your latest rabbit hole," he said, turning his attention back to the computer in his small office. "Do you mind? I'm busy."

"Aren't you concerned that the person who planted the bomb that was meant to kill you will try again?"

He didn't answer for a while, to the point that I was wondering if we should just leave.

"I'm more careful nowadays."

"You can't stop someone from killing you if you don't know who he is."

Tendrix was silent again.

"Then again," I added, "maybe you do know."

He swiveled his office chair to look at us.

"I figure you guys are probably right. A drug runner thinks I saw him and was sending me a warning."

"A pipe bomb inside your wheelhouse is more than a warning," Matt said.

"Why are you guys here again?"

"We've found a different rabbit hole," I said. "Tell us, doesn't it seem strange that all the murder victims are members of the Crab County Sportsmen's Club?"

"It's not strange in a semi-rural county like this, where just about everyone hunts and fishes."

"I didn't say it's strange that they're all sportsmen, but that they're all members of the same club—one that's mostly for socializing."

"I'm not getting the distinction."

"When people get together socially, gossip can create hurt feelings."

"I wish you'd get to the point."

"Did you have an affair with Chief Dullart's wife?"

Tendrix tried to keep his composure, but his eyes widened in surprise.

"I know some members of the club," Matt said. "There's a persistent rumor about your affair. And everyone is still talking about how the chief's wife threw a glass of wine in your face."

The face in question became red, and Tendrix turned back to his computer.

"The chief was the constant butt of jokes," Matt continued. "Look at how Max Massey went so far as to humiliate him during his press conference. Did Alfini and Higgles tease him? What about Holstein?"

"If you're implying the chief killed them because they teased him, you're crazy."

"His wife cheated on him in Pigsknuckle, Arkansas," I said. "A bunch of people got beat up. Some even turned up dead. The man has serious anger-control issues. His ego is as fragile as an eggshell, and he doesn't handle perceived injuries to his honor very well, does he?"

"No. I guess not."

"Didn't any of the club members make the connection when the guys who teased the chief ended up dead?"

"That crazy environmentalist dude killed them. Everyone knows that. The police arrested him, after all."

"I'm sure the chief planted the evidence in the suspect's home."

"How do you know?" Tendrix asked. "Can you prove that?"

"We don't have to. We only need to prove that the chief was the murderer."

"Do you have security video of the night before your boat was bombed?" Matt asked.

"The camera lenses were spray-painted over."

"Did you get a glimpse of the guy before he started spraying?"

"He wore a ski mask."

"Was he fat?"

"Guys, you can't make accusations like that about the chief of police," Tendrix said wearily. "It's irresponsible and dangerous."

"Yes, dangerous. Did he bomb your boat because you had an affair with his wife, or because you know he killed the other men?"

"Or both?" Matt asked.

"Get out of here before I call the police. I'll tell them what you were asking me about. I'll tell the chief."

A reporter and a shopkeeper-slash-witch had no leverage to force him to talk. I had to turn to the heavy weaponry, even though it seemed unfair.

Subtly, when he wasn't looking, I sprinkled the herb-and-powder mixture onto Tendrix's floor. Next, I recited the words of the spell.

"Go on, get out of here," he said angrily.

Time to throw my Hail-Mary pass. I silently mouthed the invocation.

"After his bomb failed to kill you, did the chief come to an agreement with you?" I asked. "Like, if you don't tell anyone you suspect he bombed your boat, he won't investigate that you're involved with Rivas's drug smuggling?"

Tendrix's facial muscles contorted as he appeared to undergo a colossal internal struggle. The spell must be working. It activated a person's natural urge to unburden himself and stop hiding the truth. My question, though, was one his conscious brain really didn't want to answer. Which part of him would win?

"Rivas lied to me," he said in a choked voice. "When his boat was being repaired after the feds shot at him—"

"The *feds* shot at him?" Matt asked.

"Yeah. The DEA almost caught him during a drug run. I hadn't known that when he asked to borrow my personal boat so he could fish and not leave his customers in the lurch. I didn't think for a minute that he'd use my boat for drug runs. I guess someone at the Jellyfish Beach P.D. saw him and got my boat's registration number. So, the chief knew it was my boat. I could've said I didn't give Rivas permission to use my boat for illegal activities, but it wouldn't take away the stain to my reputation and my business. The chief offered to look the other way in exchange for me not telling anyone he might have been involved in the bombing of my boat."

He continued to struggle with himself. I repeated the spell's invocation under my breath.

Tendrix continued, "When I found out my insurance would cover the bomb damage, I thought, 'what the heck?' and agreed to Dullart's deal. I didn't want the police chief as my enemy anymore. That can ruin your life. And now, I have leverage over him, so I'm safe."

"Did you suspect the chief murdered those men?"

"He overheard them making jokes about him and his wife more than once. He probably heard about it from others, too. Leslie and I had our affair before I knew Chief Dullart. She moved here a few months before him, and we met. Things escalated fast. I knew she was married, but not that her husband was going to be the police chief! When I found out, I broke it off with her.

"I knew he had a violent temper, just not this bad," he went on. "After the executive committee voted to kick him out of the club—that's when the killings began. When Holstein was killed at the boat ramp, I didn't know what to make of it. But when Alfini and Higgles were shot with their own bang sticks, I got suspicious. Then, I was targeted with a bomb. And when Massey was whacked, I was pretty sure Dullart was responsible."

"Did you tell him that?"

"Do you think I'm crazy? Heck no."

"Will you testify in court about this?"

"I don't know."

Yes, the truth spell was still working. But I think we had enough information.

"Matt, let's go. Thank you, Captain."

"Man," Matt said while we were driving. "This sure is messed up. We can't trust the local police. Let's go straight to the FBI or the Florida Department of Law Enforcement about the murders. It sounds like the DEA already has the drug investigation under control."

"Unfortunately, it's our word against the chief's."

"If we can get the FBI or FDLE to investigate this, hopefully they'll find the forensic evidence they need to make a case. If we're lucky, Tendrix will do the right thing and testify."

"I hate to admit it," I said, "but things would be so much easier if Frank really had been the murderer. Or even the munuanes."

Strobe lights filled my rearview mirror. The police car turned on its siren.

"I wasn't speeding," I said as I pulled to the side of the road.

"Didn't you kind of roll through that last stop sign?" Matt said, looking behind us.

In my mirror, I saw the officer step out of the patrol car.

"Oh, my," I said. "It's the chief."

"It has to be a coincidence."

"Unless Tendrix called him and unburdened himself before the truth spell wore off."

Matt looked at me with horror.

Chief Dullart tapped on my window. I lowered it.

"That was mighty reckless the way you were driving," he said.

"What do you mean? I wasn't speeding."

"You *were* speeding. And driving erratically, like you're on drugs or fleeing from a crime." He raised his voice. "Why are you resisting arrest?"

What was he talking about? Then, I noticed he was wearing a body camera.

He stepped back from the car, angling the camera away from the interior.

"Don't touch that gun!" he shouted. "The suspect has a gun!"

He pulled out his pistol, and before I knew what I was doing, my car shot away from him, tires squealing.

"What the—" Matt said.

I needed time to conjure a protection spell—more than the few seconds I had before Dullart killed us under the false claim that he did it to stop us from shooting him.

"You can't outrun the police," Matt whined. "Especially not in this piece of junk."

"Take that back. This car has been loyal to me forever."

"Literally forever."

The fact that I needed to use magic every five thousand miles or so to keep my Toyota from going into rigor mortis gave me an idea. After the protection spell was completed with enough strength to withstand a bullet—for a limited time—I cast a spell that put a little extra pep in my car.

My speed picked up, giving me more distance between my taillights and the chief's car with its siren blaring. However, while my car was faster, it didn't mean my driving skills increased enough to compensate.

I narrowly missed a truck slowing for a turn. We needed to get further from town and away from other vehicles. I turned off the main road and headed west toward the boondocks.

Matt had gotten over his panic and was now on the phone with his editor, blurting out everything we knew and suspected about Chief Dullart. It was a good idea, because we could evade the police for only so long, and we needed to fight back with the truth. Matt wisely didn't mention the drug smuggling. That was a whole other can of worms that didn't need to be opened right now.

"Tell him to call the FBI," I said.

"He has them on the other line."

"There's another patrol car right behind the chief's."

We were now on a road that was straight as an arrow. The only thing keeping us from being caught was the speed at which I was driving.

Taking advantage of the straight road, I made a phone call to Mrs. Lupis. My jaw clenched with frustration when I got her voicemail.

"Please help us, however you can," I begged. I described the situation and where we were headed. I tried Mr. Lopez's number and got voicemail, too. I left the same message with him. What else could I do?

My car shuddered.

"That doesn't sound good," Matt said.

And then, up ahead, strobe lights were flashing.

"Oh, my. Is the road blocked?"

No, the third patrol car blocked the other lane. In my lane

were spike strips stretched across the asphalt to puncture my tires.

"Oh, my!"

I tried to avoid the strips by swerving off the road, but I lost control. My car flopped down an embankment and landed in a swampy area near a forest.

We were lucky we didn't end up in one of South Florida's ubiquitous roadside canals. That could have been fatal.

Yes, instead of drowning, we'd be shot.

"Run for those trees," I said. "And stick near me to stay inside the protection bubble."

The ground was covered in ankle-deep water. Which made running unbearably difficult. We half-walked, half-waded toward the trees with a disgusting sucking sound each time we pulled a foot up.

Car doors slammed on the road behind us.

"Remember, they're armed," the chief shouted. I would recognize his froggy voice anywhere.

"Stop with your hands up!" commanded a voice over a loudspeaker.

I knew the chief didn't want us to stop. He wanted us dead because of what we knew.

Of course we didn't stop.

The amplified voice ordered us to stop again, but before he finished his sentence, a shot rang out.

It wasn't a warning shot. Something whizzed past my ear like a supersonic bee.

"Raise your hands to show we're unarmed, but keep going," I called to Matt.

We did so, which made it even more awkward pulling our

feet from the sucking mud and plunging them back in. At least we were close to the trees.

Two more retorts behind us. Bark flew from the tree just ahead of me. I felt a tug in the protection bubble, which meant it deflected a bullet.

The question was, how long could I keep up the power of the spell? As I grew physically exhausted, my loss of energy would weaken the bubble.

When we finally entered the woods, the officers were firing almost steadily, but they quickly stopped. I chanced a look behind me to see the chief making his way across the field alone. Two officers remained beside the roadway.

It occurred to me we were beyond the city limits, and this was the jurisdiction of the county Sheriff. His deputies should have been here by now, but they weren't. The chief must have ordered his men to keep this within the family.

"Why is the chief coming by himself?" Matt asked.

"So, he can summarily execute us with no witnesses and claim it was self-defense."

"Yeah. I was afraid of that."

For an overweight guy, the chief was making good time. I turned my focus to finding a way through the woods without a trail. And where exactly were we supposed to go?

When we reached a small river that blocked our path, my despair overwhelmed me.

And then, the chief showed up.

"How did you get here so fast?" Matt asked.

"Wh-wh-what are you sayin'?" Chief Dullart panted like a steam locomotive. "You think I'm too fat to move fast?"

"Well, yes."

The chief's already red and sweaty face turned darker red. Wouldn't it be nice if he would just drop dead of a heart attack right now before he killed us?

"I heard you two radicals were sniffing around in my business," the chief said amid his panting. "And you," he pointed at Matt, "you scruffy Bolshevik, were making fun of me during my press conference."

"See? I told you," Matt said to me.

"You two don't understand. A man's honor is all he has in the end. I must preserve my honor, no matter what it takes. You two have been hearing lies from my enemies—from the little maggots who are jealous of me, so they disrespect me, hoping to knock me down a few pegs. Well, I have to show them they're wrong. That I'm a much bigger man than they are. I have to punish them for their disrespect. Because without honor, I have nothing. *Nothing!* Do you understand?"

"Absolutely," Matt said. "And for the record, I've always respected you, Chief. So, Missy and I are going to head back to Jellyfish Beach right now. If that's okay with you, sir?"

"Shut up, you commie."

The chief, having finally regained his wind, held his pistol in two hands, moving it back and forth between aiming at my head and Matt's.

I had been feverishly building my sleep spell. It's faster than the immobility spell, and I obviously needed to knock the chief out before he pulled the trigger.

"You losers have no idea how superior I am to you. Get ready to—"

He fell backward against a cypress tree, hitting it with his back and sliding down the trunk until he sat on the ground, leaning against the tree, his legs splayed out before him. His snores scared away all the nearby birds.

"Thanks for the sleep spell," Matt said, "but there are two other cops back there. Can you enchant them, too?"

"They're too far away."

"How are we going to find safety when we're on foot?"

Even though our immediate deaths had been avoided, I fell back into despair. Because Matt was right—we would be caught.

With no other options, we swam across the river, then followed the river's course through the forest. We must have been in the Wikowackee Preserve. If we escaped the police, we would probably perish from the elements.

A couple of hours later, shouts came from a distance behind us.

"They're catching up," Matt said. "And the chief might be awake."

A sense of defeat overwhelmed me. I was so exhausted, I couldn't go on.

But soon, I heard the slap of a paddle approaching from around a river bend.

The munuane was atop an extra-large paddle board. He came straight toward us. Based on his large size and gray-flecked hair, it was the patriarch.

My guess was that Mrs. Lupis and Mr. Lopez asked Angela to use her magic to find our location and ask the munuane to rescue us.

The eyes on his knees looked at us sympathetically. He gestured for us to come aboard.

Matt and I sat awkwardly on the board like amateurs. The

munuane stood between us, with me in the front, facing our rescuer, and Matt in the back. He paddled quickly, taking us downstream in the direction from which he had come.

I made eye contact with his knees and smiled warmly, trying to show gratitude for him saving us. Warm vibes came to me in return.

Matt, sitting behind the creature, still had fear in his eyes. Once again, he had almost lost his life. He never would have gotten this deep into the murder mystery if it hadn't been for me.

Yeah, I shouldn't get involved with anyone while my life was about chasing monsters. It would be too dangerous and unfair for them. Even a guy like Matt, who kept coming back for more of Missy's madness.

After we went around a bend, the crashing of a large creature struggling through the undergrowth came from where we had just been.

The creature cursed in a rumbling voice that was strangely high-pitched.

Yes, the creature was a human. One who had taken many lives and would hopefully end up in captivity soon.

CHAPTER 26

BLACK MAGIC WOMEN

I stood with Matt in the rear parking lot of the Jellyfish Beach Police Station. Our breakfast together had been rushed because Matt received a tip from Detective Shortle that Carrascal was arriving soon to give a statement to the police and the DEA. It wasn't a pivotal event, but it was newsworthy, so Matt, a photographer from the *Journal*, and a television news crew from WARP were there to watch the drug lord arrive.

The reason the visit was newsworthy was the fact that Raul Rivas had been arrested two days ago by the DEA. And apparently, he had tried to implicate Carrascal. The drug lord was the bigger fish, but the DEA would have a much trickier time landing him.

"In all my years covering the city, I've never seen so much activity surrounding the police department," Matt said. "And now, they don't have a chief."

Chief Dullart had been arrested a day before Rivas had.

Believe it or not, Captain Tendrix had done the right thing and was cooperating with investigators, according to Matt.

"It sounds like they're building a decent case against Dullart," he said. "DNA evidence found in the alligator hunters' boat matches his. As for the murder at the boat ramp, it turns out while there was no security camera pointed at the location where Holstein was murdered, there was security footage of the parking lot. Detective Shortle acquired it, but it was supposedly later destroyed—by Chief Dullart, I'm sure. The Parks and Recreation Department had a backup drive with the footage. Shortle confirmed that the chief's personal car was in the parking lot at the same time the autopsy had determined was the victim's time of death."

"Oh, my."

"Massey, the Thong Man, obviously wasn't digging up turtle eggs. A witness saw him walking up the beach with another man, who they identified as the chief, toward the location where Massey's body was found. He was killed next to the nest, and the chief probably dug up the eggs to make it look like the victim had done it."

"What about the bomb on the *Sea Fog*?" I asked.

"That's a tricky one. As we already heard, the security camera at the marina that faced the *Sea Fog* had been spray painted by someone with the chief's build on the night prior to when the bomb went off. Captain Tendrix told the police he believes the chief did it."

"Looks like even when you're the chief of police, you can't destroy or bury all the evidence against you."

"And you can plant evidence to incriminate someone else very easily. Shortle interviewed the officers who went with the chief to arrest Frank Fitzwhizzle. And, really, how often would a chief go to arrest a suspect? The officers said the chief was only concerned with finding Frank's laptop and bullied him into revealing his password. The laptop was signed into the evidence room later than it should have been. It had a journal allegedly written by Frank with photos of the victims."

"The chief created it himself?"

"That's what it looks like. There are ways to prove it wasn't created by Frank."

"It sounds like the chief planned to pin it on Frank all along."

Matt nodded. "He killed because of his rage over being dishonored, but was very methodical about it."

"And imaginative, too, tying the deaths together with an eco-terrorism theme."

The journalists grew excited when the large black SUV arrived in the parking lot. Not every tiny city like Jellyfish Beach can boast having a big-time drug lord. The reporter and cameraman from WARP pushed up to the rear doors as Carrascal and his lawyer got out. A bodyguard jumped out of the front passenger seat and tried to block them. Matt and I remained closer to the building as his photographer snapped rapid shots of Carrascal approaching the door.

"Mr. Carrascal, does Raul Rivas work for you?" Matt shouted.

Carrascal looked up. He recognized us and smiled. He and his team walked past us, and I blurted out a question in a voice low enough that only those nearby would hear.

"Why did you let the munuanes stay in your homes?"

He stopped, surprised, then smiled again.

"When I was a boy, a munuane saved me from drowning. I will never forget."

They passed us and went into a back door held open by an officer.

"Do they allow kazoos in prison?" I asked Matt. A drug lord was most likely the only person who could get away with playing the kazoo without being killed by his fellow prisoners.

"I don't know. But I bet it will be a long time before this guy ends up in prison."

THE BELL above the botanica's door tinkled. I looked up from behind the counter, expecting to see one of our regular customers. Instead, it was a tall, dorky guy with a long face and eyes too close together. He wore a Renaissance-era tunic and tights, similar to what Don Mateo sometimes appeared in.

I don't care how weird Florida is. Men simply don't wear tights, unless they're a ghost or attending a Renaissance festival.

The man, of course, was Tim Tissy, who fancied calling himself Lord Arseton of the Knights Simplar.

"Just who I didn't want to see in our store again," I said. I wasn't too good at customer service. "You must be out on bail for your false imprisonment charges."

"I see your store is empty of customers as usual," he said with a sneer and a lame attempt at an upper-class English accent.

"The place will be hopping during the lunch rush."

"Is the zombie here?"

"No, Carl is not." Thank goodness. I didn't need Lord Dork harassing him. "Why are you here?"

"I wish to ask you about a couple of matters. Not that I expect you to cooperate. A monster has been spotted in a waterway nearby—a hairy creature that doesn't match any known species."

"I haven't heard any such thing," I lied.

"Your Cryptid Society hasn't heard?"

I shook my head. I didn't know how he had heard about the Friends of Cryptids Society or a munuane sighting.

He regarded me suspiciously.

"I believe you know what I'm talking about. My knights will hunt this creature and slay it."

Not on my watch. As soon as he left, I would call Angela and ask her to warn the munuanes about weird dudes in tights.

"And I've also heard credible reports of black magic being practiced in Jellyfish Beach. Are you involved?" His eyes roved the store as if he hoped to spot products labeled "for black magic."

"Really?" I asked with great interest. "Tell me what you heard."

"You're interrogating *me*?"

"Yes. I'm just as concerned about it as you are."

Taken off guard by my attitude, Lord Arseton opened up.

"It seems there is a coven of black-magic witches forming here in Jellyfish Beach," he explained. "You know how the Knights Simplar feels about witches like you. Those who practice black magic are even more evil in our minds."

"They should be. I've heard that a woman named Harriet Chase is dabbling in the black arts."

264

He was surprised I gave him a name. But I wouldn't mind Harriet being tormented by Lord Arseton and his goons. After all, the enemy of my enemy, and all that.

Really, the witch tried to kill me with the toothpaste of death. She deserved whatever Arseton had in mind for her.

"Where does she live?" he asked. He seemed as surprised as I was that I had cooperated.

"You can find her yourself. What will you do with her?"

He laughed. At that moment, his dorkiness turned from amusing to evil.

"The cure for witches is as old as civilization. We must rid the earth of her and her kind. Surely, you've heard of burning witches at the stake?"

"Don't be an idiot. You'll go to prison for life, if you don't get the death penalty."

"The death penalty is what she deserves for dabbling in black magic and consorting with Satan."

"What are you talking about? You guys worship a demon."

"We follow an angel. Myron is our guide and moral compass."

"He's a demon who has blinded you to what he is."

"Don't insult our beliefs, witch. You don't appear to practice the dark arts, but you're still a witch who protects monsters. If you're not careful, you'll be next on the stake."

He gave a little snort of satisfaction, as if he had won something over me, and left the botanica.

This guy was such a freak. I didn't understand him—how he could be so self-righteous, dorky, and evil at the same time? I wished they hadn't let him out on bail.

He was correct that I protected monsters, at least ones who

weren't too deadly to humans. But Lord Arseton was worse than all of them. Humans are actually the scariest monsters of all. Thankfully, this one was too much of a dunderhead to be lethal.

But what if he kills Harriet?

I now regretted giving him her name. How could I allow anyone to be burned at the stake?

Not having her phone number, I emailed her with a warning to be on the lookout for a man named Tim Tissy who called himself Lord Arseton. I included his physical description and mentioned that he had followers.

Then, I returned my focus to the minutia of running a retail store. My life had been so out of balance after the murders and dealing with the munuanes, it was good to return to normal.

Normal being a relative term for me. Another Catholic saint figurine on the shelf animated itself and tried to make me feel guilty.

"You've actually been inside of a church twice in recent weeks," said Saint Sebastian. "Was it really so difficult?"

I tried not to laugh at the earnest expression on the statuette's sloppily painted face. It surely hadn't been made in the USA.

"Maybe I don't show up every Sunday, but I rid the church of evil black magic. So there."

His face returned to inert ceramic. He must have realized it was fruitless to debate me in my present mood.

In other matters, Frank Fitzwhizzle was released from jail when former Chief Dullart was formally indicted for murder and attempted murder.

The Friends of Cryptids Society of the Americas was blessedly quiet. Detective Shortle didn't ask me again about any secret groups. Hopefully, my fears of the Society being unveiled were overblown. And my domestic life was peaceful, aside from the occasional quarrel between my cats and a certain iguana.

But I couldn't shake the feeling that I had done something terribly wrong in revealing Harriet's name to Lord Arseton. She never replied to my email, and I was worried.

There was no council or guild of magic practitioners in this area to help me with this matter. My cousin lived in a city with a Magic Guild that both regulated and protected witches. The guild there banned black magic, but at the same time would save any witch who was persecuted. I wished we had a guild here.

I had to take matters into my own hands. I drove to Harriet's apartment, hoping to find her there so I could warn her about Arseton, in case she hadn't read my email.

When I walked to her front door, I was fully encased inside a protection bubble with extra power added to it. I rang the doorbell and prepared to run at the first sight of the toothpaste of death.

She didn't answer. I rang the bell once more. Apparently, she wasn't home. I was stepping away from her door when it opened.

"Oh, it's you." She wasn't as hostile as before. "You're a witch, aren't you? I sensed it in you when you were here last time."

"Yes, I am. I dropped by today in person because you didn't respond to my email warning you about the crazy cult."

"Oh, yes. Sorry, I'm horrible with emails. Thank you for the warning, but I'm not at all worried."

"You should be. These guys are losers, but they're still dangerous."

"Do they practice magic?"

"Not really, but they serve a demon who is bad news. They think it's an angel, though, so they believe they're righteous in everything they do. They consider themselves the soldiers of God, but they're really a cult."

"They sound like good allies for Nature Under the Spotlight."

"Normally, allies don't want to burn you at the stake."

"Oh." She giggled. "They do sound like nut jobs."

Spoken by someone who should know.

"Yes," I said. "You should watch out for them. And, um, don't take this the wrong way, but why are you being nice to me? You tried to kill me the last time I was here."

"Aww, that spell wouldn't have killed you. Well, maybe if you stood right in its path. It was meant simply to frighten you because you were treating me like a murder suspect. I'm so pleased to hear on the local news that the murders have been solved and environmental groups are no longer suspects. I'd invite you in, but I'm preparing for my first coven sabbath."

"No worries." Not that I would ever enter this woman's home after what she did to me, despite her cheerful demeanor.

"Are you interested in joining us? No pressure—you can just sit in and observe. You'll see that black magic is so much more effective than any of your silly games."

"No, thanks. Black magic is not my cup of tea."

"We'll soon have one of the most powerful sorceresses in the Southeast training us."

"Sorry, but . . ." Remembering the note from my mother, a

troubling idea popped into my mind. "Just curious—what's her name?"

"Ruth Bent."

My heart sank with the confirmation. There was no mistaking who their new trainer was going to be. Ruth Bent was one of my mother's aliases.

Yes, she was back in my life. No doubt bringing chaos and destruction and a lot of emotional blackmail.

Why me?

WHAT'S NEXT

Book 4 of Monsters of Jellyfish Beach: *My Funny Frankenstein*

A monstrous murder.

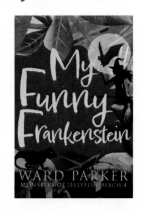

I'm Missy Mindle, middle-aged witch, sometimes nurse, and woman up to her eyeballs in monsters. Now, I must solve the murder of a voodoo sorcerer. The victim, along with a fantastically wealthy vampire, had been using magic and alchemy to create freakish, unnatural creatures.

Speaking of which, would you like to adopt a cat-monkey looking for a forever home? I didn't think so.

There are many folks with motives to murder the sorcerer, such as his partner, the vampire, as well as several disgruntled customers. Or, who knows? Maybe he'd created a Frankenstein's monster that killed its creator.

Anything is possible. Especially when you live in Jellyfish Beach.

Dive into a wacky world of murder, magic, and mayhem with the "Monsters of Jellyfish Beach." Get it on Amazon or at wardparker.com

GET A FREE E-BOOK

Sign up for my newsletter, and get *A Ghostly Touch*, a Memory Guild novella, for free, offered exclusively to my newsletter subscribers. Darla reads the memories of a young woman, murdered in the 1890s, whose ghost begins haunting Darla, looking for justice. As a subscriber, you'll be the first to know about my new releases and lots of free book promotions. The newsletter is delivered only a couple of times a month. No spam at all, and you can unsubscribe at any time. Get it at wardparker.com

Acknowledgments

I wish to thank my loyal readers, who give me a reason to write more every day. I'm especially grateful to Sharee Steinberg and Shelley Holloway for all your editing and proofreading brilliance. To my A Team (you know who you are), thanks for reading and reviewing my ARCs, as well as providing good suggestions. And to my wife, Martha, thank you for your moral support, Beta reading, and awesome graphic design!

ABOUT THE AUTHOR

Ward is also the author of the Memory Guild midlife paranormal mystery thrillers, as well as the Freaky Florida series, set in the same world as Monsters of Jellyfish Beach, with Missy, Matt, Agnes, and many other familiar characters.

Ward lives in Florida with his wife, several cats, and a demon who wishes to remain anonymous.

Connect with him on social media: Twitter (@wardparker), Facebook (wardparkerauthor), BookBub, Goodreads, or check out his books at wardparker.com

PARANORMAL BOOKS BY WARD PARKER

Freaky Florida Humorous Paranormal Novels
Snowbirds of Prey
Invasive Species
Fate Is a Witch
Gnome Coming
Going Batty
Dirty Old Manatee
Gazillions of Reptilians
Hangry as Hell (novella)
Books 1-3 Box Set

The Memory Guild Midlife Paranormal Mystery Thrillers

A Magic Touch (also available in audio)
The Psychic Touch (also available in audio)
A Wicked Touch (also available in audio)
A Haunting Touch
The Wizard's Touch
A Witchy Touch
A Faerie's Touch
The Goddess's Touch
The Vampire's Touch
An Angel's Touch
A Ghostly Touch (novella)
Books 1-3 Box Set (also available in audio)

Monsters of Jellyfish Beach Paranormal Mystery Adventures

The Golden Ghouls
Fiends With Benefits
Get Ogre Yourself
My Funny Frankenstein

Made in United States
North Haven, CT
02 October 2023

42292961R00169